Blue Cat

Stephen Pryde-Jarman

Falling Star Books

|

If I hadn't taken four sleeping pills to kill the day and forget I had lost another job to a robot, who did it five times faster and twice as correct, this story wouldn't have happened. I'd had a blow-up because of it and was told to see a psychiatrist. I had tossed and twisted all night like there were gremlins under my bed. But when I opened my eyes and looked at my pale chest with the two lone hairs, the word that came to me was not 'scrawny.' That morning, I liked my body. It was neat and compact and not hairy like some I'd seen out in the world. I took a long, luxurious breath, the air fresh as if dusted with a golden chemical. I yawned, stretched, and scratched where the two hairs were, then looked around.

A blue cat was on the sill of the large open circular window.

'Is that a cat?' I said, with a hint of a morning croak. The sound of my voice asked another question. *'Is it blue?'*

I suppressed the second question. I was in too good a mood to let it worry me. If I had gone mad, three cheers for insanity. Besides, there were many natural explanations for the cat's unconventional colour. The day before, I had seen a nurse leading two blue poodles down the street.

'They aren't dye-jobs,' she told anyone who passed her. 'They're mutations!'

And weren't there other animals coloured blue? The poison dart frog? Though I recalled, the poison dart frog's hue was because of a fungus. There wasn't any fungus on the burnished bundle of benignity on my windowsill.

I connected the cat with my newborn sense of well-being from the first. If there was going to be a new era in my life, it was a good idea to have a symbol for it - a symbol that matched the clear blue sky of my psyche.

'I'm going to call you Zen, 'I whispered, without lifting my head from the pillow. 'Here, kitty, kitty, kitty.'

The invitation sounded silly once said out loud. The cat dropped its plump body from the windowsill and trotted toward me like a soft-shod miniature horse. There was an abnormal increase in the calm and joy inside me. The cat disappeared under the angle of the bedside table. Then a little blue face came over the edge, and two tiny blue paws placed themselves beside it.

'You're a strange little thing. Where did you come from?'

The little face tipped upward, and two blue eyes sparkled.

'From upstairs?' I chuckled at my skill in interpreting the cat's movements. 'Why not stay with me for a while?'

It was a strange and attractive cat face. The ears were large, the forehead high, the nose-button lost in fur, the whiskers straight-forward, and the mouth carried the suggestion of a pout. And it was blue.

Thinking about the word 'he,' I wondered about Zen's sex. The fat tummy was suggestive. Yet, I was sure the cat was a male. Zen smiled again. I put out a tentative hand and jerked it back when a little paw flicked out at it. I repeated the gesture. The little foot touched my middle finger. I stroked the silken paw - no hint of claws.

'Now we're friends,' I said. The cat sprang onto the bed. A furry cheek brushed mine with casual, feline friendliness. Tears stung my eyes, enough to brim the lids but not to run over. What a lonely old fool I must be. A cat made me cry. But it was genuine enough. All my life, I had been fading. My parents seemed warm at first, but I soon sensed their boredom. School had been full of promise at one point, with infinite vistas of knowledge and aca-demic brotherhood opening up. But too often, the information superhighway ended with signs saying 'restricted' or 'closed to a small plump man called Maurice.' a shame because Maurice is my name.

I'd had friends, too, and had been in love with girls. Even that had become washed out and worthless. And the endless business of being beaten out of jobs by robots. The only thing robots couldn't do, it seemed, was sit in foxholes and get shot at. That was one place where I recalled no mechanical competition.

Yes, it had been an empty, purposeless life, but at the same time, even those thoughts couldn't mar my current happiness.

The cat was marching around the bed, inspecting my naked body.

'That's going too far. Give me some privacy!' I chuckled as I swung out of bed, grabbing a light robe. I hummed a couple of bars of 'Luck be a Lady' and did a shuffling step that brought the cat hurrying over to play tag with my toes.

'Where *did* you come from?' I repeated and turned toward the window. My gaze fell on the near-empty dispenser of sleeping pills, and for a moment, the eerie doubt came back: mightn't that morning's overdose have triggered all of this? After all, this cat wasn't typical. My inexplicable happiness was altogether too much like a world of godlike perfection to be real. Was this heaven? Was I dead? But I was at the window, experiencing a new twist in my mood.

Love Incorporated bought my building as social housing for tax relief. They cut its vast rooms into tiny sleeping cells. It kept at least one feature from its glory days: the large circular windows formed of two sheets of polarizing glass, the inner of which rotated, allowing a person to blacken their window. An unusual luxury touch was that the windows opened, swinging on pivots at the top and bottom.

The grey wall across the courtyard from my window, with its rows of ominous portholes, was the grimmest sight in the world. If I leaned out a little, it seemed to me I could imagine my way through that grey wall as if it were a cloud. Through to the multiple textures of pitiful, admirable, ridiculous human lives in the cubicles. The two-fifths happy people, the nine-tenths sad ones, the ones who nursed fears and frustrations, the ones who hammered fears and frustrations into armour, and the boy pretending the blacked-out window was the porthole of an intergalactic liner.

A hand came out of a porthole three floors up and shook something - or nothing - from a dustpan. Coincidence, of course. I interpreted the event as a confirmation of my new outgoingness. The smile left my lips, and I thought of another aspect of the opposite wall.

Ms Celeste was stood at her window and inspecting an assortment of wispy lingerie. This auspicious situation would have held me helpless for twenty minutes or more. But I found I could look at her and look away without the faintest gnawing worry I might miss something.

'Prrrt!' A feathery, furry ball came into my hand, and I looked down at Zen's blue face framed by my curving forefinger and thumb.

'What do you want, Zen?'

Zen ducked out of the cupped hand with a twist. He let me rub his forehead and ear and put his front paws on the windowsill. I advanced my hand, so it circled the cat's chest. I didn't want Zen to get back out on the little ledge. I didn't wish him to leave me at all, though something told me I wouldn't be able to stop it if it wanted to go.

With a shamefaced satisfaction, it occurred to me that Love Incorporated forbid all pets in the building. Zen's owner wouldn't be able to do anything open about getting the refined feline back.

But Zen seemed to have no intention of leaving. He hopped to the floor and looked at me.

'Prrrt!'

'Want something to eat?'

'Prrrt-part!'

I took a mental inventory of my fridge and the cranberry concentrate on the second shelf. Inappropriate and yet something assured me it would be perfect for Zen. It was a dark-red marble swelled to a glistening ruby golf ball at the touch of water. At another inward prompting, the syrupy contents of a vitamin capsule poured over it. The last ingredient smelled rank indeed, and by the time I set the odd sundae on the floor, I was doubtful. But Zen examined it with signs of approval, mewing in eagerness. But, instead of eating it, the blue cat looked at me. The little chap wanted to eat in private.

'Fine,' I said. 'I'll take a shower and leave you to it.'

Stepping inside the bathroom, I set the shower controls to alternate between tepid and warm. Instead, it alternated between icy and steaming, so I leapt out with a shriek. But the incident didn't even scratch my mood. I towelled myself and sang:

Luck, be a lady tonight.

Luck, be a lady tonight.

Luck, if you've ever been a lady, to begin with.

Luck, be a lady tonight.

I came out of the bathroom neat, clean, shaved, and sober, and I didn't care who knew it. I slipped on a white shirt, trousers, moccasins, and jacket. I explained my feelings to Zen, who had cleaned every bit of his colourful meal.

'I've always been three-quarters dead. But not anymore. I'm through with being scared and bored with a soon-to-be-invented robot breathing down my neck. I'm going out to find out what life is all about. I'm going to have adventures. I'm going to get a living. And it's all thanks to you!'

Zen fluffed his gleaming blue fur.

I wondered what time it was. My watch had gone the day before, only five months after having the battery replaced. I stuck my head out the window and looked up the dizzy grey walls to a ribbon of blue sky.

I scooped up Zen without the thought of leaving him. But the cat sprang from my arms and made for the hall door, looking back as if to say, 'I'm right there with you, babe, I'm game for any adventure.'

Side by side, man and cat. We walked to the stairs and down to level twenty-eight. There I ran into Celeste, heading for the snack bar.

'Hello, Celeste,' I said.

She glanced at me sideways and smiled a small fluffy smile. 'You know my name?' she said in a foreign accent I couldn't quite place.

'I asked the desk robot who the beautiful girl was in 28-303a.'

She tittered with a flirtatious contempt. 'You don't talk to desk robot. It won't give out names unless you have a master key.'

'I have a way with robots,' I explained. 'I win their confidence with small talk.'

'I must watch you.' she turned her head and ran her hand through her hair.

'Do you like my blue cat?' I said.

'Blue cat!' Celeste looked down and up. 'Where?'

Zen wasn't anywhere in sight. A hunk of ice materialized inside my chest. 'I've got to go,' I said. 'I hope we'll meet again, Celeste.'

I raced to the corridor. Zen was waiting in front of the elevator.

'Don't do that,' I said. 'You'll give me a heart attack.'

||

Alta Brea Crescent snarled. Out there, people were drowning, mutilated, cut by breaking glass, mashed against steering wheels or under heavy tires. People were being beaten and strangled, robbed and strangled, or cheated and strangled. People were greedy, sick, tired, frantic with loneliness and sorrow and fear, irritable, spiteful, fiery, intimidated. A charged-up electric car swerved close to the curb to remove a triangular chunk from the rump of a large man who had been too slow in skittering to safety. A second look showed it was not a large man but a thin man in a balloon suit. It deflated, and he sat in the limp folds on the curb and sobbed. Balloon suits were of no absolute protection to pedestrians, except by increasing the target, but they continued to catch on. During the last war, the government had sold one pumped full of hydrogen, a shield against neutrons, they said, until a couple of small but unpleasant explosions in crowded shelters caused a crackdown.

The street continued to growl deep in its throat - it had two lower levels. They composed the hum of electrics, the subterranean rumble of heavier traffic, the yak-yak of competing conversations, and the nervous shuffle of feet that was intensified here because most of the women's feet were on platforms three to ten inches high.

Neither the growl nor the snarl disturbed me. I had my earplugs tucked in, my face fixed straight ahead, my eyes questing for cars, which jumped curbs. I wanted to drink it all in, to see the things I'd always been blind to, to note the anxious but apathetic expressions on the faces of the pedestrians, to sense the invisible lines of force, like marionette strings, that joined them to the world.

Zen was no more frightened of the street than I was. He scampered along close to the base of the buildings, the camouflaging blue colour of which may have explained why none of the pedestrians saw him.

A gleaming sales robot veered toward me on its silent wheels. Still, I interposed another balloon-suited man between myself and it. The balloon-suited man got a slick sales talk while I hurried around the corner after Zen, who had turned down Foppery Avenue. He glided up the sidewalk and padded across the road between the passing cars as if picking up a scent. I followed, with my heart thumping. Finally, I pulled up to an ornate cave mouth flanked with old-fashioned fluorescent posters, the largest lettering on which read:

TONIGHT!

Cleopatra The Man-Maiming Egyptian

vs

Hercules, the Bone-Crushing Misogynist.

I had no time to read the rest of the bill, for Zen was dancing along a corridor lined with photographs of menacing, half-naked wrestlers. Over the entrance doors, which would have let in a troop of Indian elephants, a broad florescent panel showed a male wrestler struggling his way out of a headlock applied by a woman the size of a bus. He didn't seem to be trying. Typically, I would be afraid of entering a wrestling venue specializing in male/female bouts. But it never occurred to me not to follow Zen.

A side corridor spilt right, short of the turnstiles and a robot ticket taker. Zen whisked into it, but I had rounded the corner after him when a long, boneless grey arm shot out of the wall and slapped itself against my middle.

'Where are you going?' a voice rasped from the wall. 'Take a hike, you lousy bum.'

Zen minced down the side corridor, lined with pink doors. I tried to go around the arm, but it extended until it stretched from wall to wall.

'You still here?' the rasping wall inquired. 'Look, if you got business with anybody....'

'I want to get my cat,' I said.

Zen had reached the end of the corridor and was peering into the last doorway. 'Here, Zen,' I called, but the blue cat took no notice.

'Means nothing to me,' the wall rasped. 'You have not given me a password or tripped any of my relays.'

Zen disappeared through the doorway.

'Please let me through to get my cat,' I said, trying to seem sincere. 'I'll be right back.'

'I am not letting anyone through,' the wall asserted. Unless they give me a password.'

An appalling spasm of fear went through me as if a light turned off inside my mind. I knew something had happened to Zen. I ducked under the grey arm and darted forward, but before I took five steps, the corridor whirled and spun me back. Looking down, I saw the elastic arm wrapped around me like a grey python while the wall grated in my ear.

'Now, I'll have to hold you here till the boss arrives.'

'Let me go. I've got to get in there!' I yelled, struggling to release my arms. All the while, I kept my eyes on the doorway through which Zen had vanished. 'Let me go!'

'What is going on?' A large, tall woman with close-cropped hair, broken nose, out-size jaw, and big bloodshot eyes stepped out of the nearest doorway. She gave me a look that conducted human sacrifices by the light of the full moon.

'What do you want?' she boomed.

'My cat ran in that room down there.' I nodded my head toward it. 'I tried to go after it, but this thing grabbed me.'

'A cat?'

'Yes, my pet cat.'

For the first time, I noticed her Egyptian robes.

'Okay,' she said after a bit. 'Let him go!'

'He didn't give me a password,' the wall complained. 'He tried to duck through. Got to hold him till the boss comes.'

'That'll be at least an hour. Let him go, you stupid robot. I am inviting him in.'

'All right, Miss Cleopatra,' the wall said. The grey arm unwrapped from around my waist and shot back into the wall.

'Now find your cat, then beat it,' the giantess said.

'Thank you,' I said, half turning to her but keeping the far doorway in the corner of my gaze. But she didn't answer, only frowned at me.

I tried not to hurry, although the corridor felt endless. I told myself nothing had happened to Zen and wished hard I could believe it. I didn't care for a big or adventurous life anymore.

I passed the woman's door, noticing heaps of untidy clothes and a stationary rubber-armed robot for wrestling practice. I came to the door at the end and hesitated. I couldn't hear a sound. I stepped inside.

The room was large, low ceilinged, and lined with lockers and benches. At the far end was a closed door flanked by two low mechanical massage tables. Their jointed rubber-fisted arms extended upward and made them look like two beetles on their backs. There were a few other pieces of apparatus, none of which I recognized, but most of the floor was empty.

In the centre of the floor was a silver box about a foot square. Staring at it, their backs turned, were two men. One was small but quick looking, dressed in a black turtleneck sweater and tight leather trousers, like a well-bred vulture. He was holding a stun gun. The other was smaller and lighter and clad in white. He had a wire leading to the box, and his whole aspect was that of a man who was struck by lightning.

I cleared my throat. The two men eyed me, then turned back to the box. I edged forward into the room, peering into the corners for Zen. I jerked back. I had stepped on a dead mouse.

Looking more closely, I saw there were half a dozen dead mice scattered around the floor. I cleared my throat again, louder, but this time the men didn't even look around. I moved forward again, tiptoeing over the dead mice.

There was a click. A tiny door opened on the top of the silver box, and a mouse catapulted out. Hitting the floor, it made off in frantic zigzags, skidding at each turn. I was expecting Zen to come darting out of a corner after it. Instead, the man in black followed the zigzags with his gun. There was no sound or flash from it, but the mouse stopped moving.

'Try to surprise me better next time, Virgil,' the man in black told his companion. 'I saw your hand move when you punched the button.'

They resumed their alert, motionless stance. Moving around them in a cautious circle, I searched for Zen. There were few likely places of concealment. The lockers reached from floor to ceiling but were all closed.

One of the dead mice twitched. Virgil put down the wire with the push-button at its end, took off his shoe, and smacked the mouse on the head.

There must have been a connection between Zen and the mice, but it was a dream connection and made little sense. I approached the motionless pair.

'Excuse me,' I said. 'Did a cat come in here?'

The words got no response.

'I beg your pardon,' I said. 'I must find my cat.'

I touched the elbow of the man in black. The response was instantaneous. A hand grabbed me, and Virgil jerked me back. His infantile features tensed into a hard mask.

'What did you just do?' he said. 'Interrupting Hercules Jones at recreation! Laying your hands on Hercules Jones! Shoving Hercules Jones around!

I was sick with fear. If only Zen were there, I could recapture my earlier mood of golden confidence.

'I was only trying to find my cat.' I quivered. 'I didn't shove him.'

'You did too! I saw you! A great big rude shove! And for a cat? Hercules Jones is the top cat around here, the only cat.' The hand holding me twisted my lapels tighter around my throat. 'You can't weasel out of what's coming to you. Hercules, what are you going to do to him?'

At long last, the man in black moved. He turned his head in its ruff of black wool and fixed on me the sad, weary smile of a man who knew it was his inescapable fate to inflict doom and punishment. He pushed out his hand until it grasped my elbow.

'Please don't,' I whispered, but a thumb dug into a nerve between my bones, and I couldn't contain a squeal of pain. The baby-faced man grinned with approval as if, at last, the improprieties were being satisfied.

Hercules Jones acted as if the squeal hadn't been loud enough and lifted his other hand. 'This is a stun-gun,' he said in a voice varnished with malice. 'Ultrasonic. I might spray your spine with it. It's set for mouse power now, but I'll step it up if necessary.'

My guts turned to water.

'You don't need to hurt me, 'I said. 'I was only looking for a cat.'

Virgil shook his head and said, 'Nosey little men doing who knows what shouldn't tell such great gigantic lies.'

Suddenly, someone shoved him ten feet. The stun-gun clattered to the floor; Hercules Jones took a quick backward spring. The blonde giantess was thundering. 'I can stand anything except bullying.'

She had slipped on a filthy short robe, embroidered in the best Egyptian style, except the figure on the back was not a pyramid or sphinx but a fire-breathing spaceship.

'Don't touch me, Cleopatra. I'm warning you!' The man in black snarled in a voice that had lost a lot of its threatening veneer, especially as he was massaging a slapped wrist.

'I beat you the first time they matched me with you,' the giantess continued. 'I beat you the night I married you. And I can do it again anytime. You *and* Virgil here,' she added. The latter's grimace was threatening but registered only spite. 'Why were you tormenting this poor little guy?'

'Tormenting?' Hercules's voice rose. 'I wasn't tormenting him. I was taking precautions. He came in here like a lunatic, not saying anything, dancing around on his toes, babbling about a cat. as if he were about to go off his nut.'

Virgil's tight-lipped face bobbed up and down in agreement. But Cleopatra wasn't at all impressed.

'He's about as dangerous as yeast spread. Why didn't you let him find his cat and get out?'

Hercules's face registered astonishment. 'Cleopatra, was it you let this imbecile in? I was wandering how he got past Old Rubber Arm. Do you mean to say you fell for his story about a cat?'

'Well, isn't there a cat?' Cleopatra demanded, scanning the room.

'How could there be?' Hercules protested, the barest note of super-iority creeping into his voice. 'You didn't see one, did you? No. And if there had been a cat, wouldn't it have been after these mice? And where could it hide in here? It couldn't have got in there!'

Cleopatra's gaze rested on the inner door. '*It's* not in there.'

'So, where is it?' Hercules finished. 'You don't suppose Virgil and I kidnapped it, do you?'

Cleopatra rubbed her battered nose. She turned to me. Her face was friendly but heavy with doubt. 'Let's hear more about that cat. What colour was it?'

'Blue,' I said. Even with the looks of disbelief on the surrounding faces, I couldn't keep myself from going on: 'Yes, bright blue. And he liked cranberry sauce. He came to me an hour ago. I called him Zen because he made me feel so good.'

There was a long silence. My spirits sank past zero.

Cleopatra laid a giant hand on my shoulder. 'Come on,' she whispered. 'You better get going.'

Hercules strode up with a wry eye on us both.

'Look, Mister,' he said to me in a concerned voice in which the mockery was still cautious, 'I had an appointment with an analyst for tonight, but you need it more than I do.'

He handed me a torn-off bit of scribe tape. I accepted it and put it in my pocket. Virgil tittered. Cleopatra whirled on him.

'Look,' she roared. 'His being a nut doesn't excuse laughing at him!'

The inner door opened, but I couldn't see inside because a tall, broad man with thick dark glasses filled it. I sensed a note of respectfulness in the other three.

'What's all the racket about?' the man demanded.

'This guy...' Virgil stopped at a quick look from Hercules.

The thick glasses flashed at me. 'One of your crazed admirers, Hercules? Get him out of here!'

'Sure thing, Mr Treacle,' said Hercules. 'Right away.'

The inner door closed, and I let Cleopatra steer me through the other.

I was lower than a worm's grave. So much so I didn't notice the odd couple coming down the corridor toward us. The man - a monk, looked saintly yet sunburned and wore orange shoes and an orange beret. The woman–a nun, looked like a young witch, with her nose and chin looking for each other. Twenty long hatpins attached a little red hat to her coarse dark hair, and she had a red skirt stiff as carpet. Both were wearing black turtlenecked sweaters.

'You'll find your little tin pot hero back there shooting mice,' snarled Cleopatra as they passed. The nun twitched her witchy nose. But the sun-burned monk looked around with elfin eyes and a benign smile. 'Joy, Cleopatra,' he admonished. 'Nothing but joy.'

The giantess looked after them for a moment, then went on. 'A couple of Hercules's intellectual fans,' she confided. 'Religious nuts, and all that goes with it.'

We turned the corner. Old Rubber Arm waggled the tip of a fingerless hand and muttered, 'No loitering.' Cleopatra silenced him with a weary, 'Shut up!'

'Now get along home,' she said. 'I don't know that I'd visit Hercules's psychiatrist if I were you.' She patted my shoulder and grinned. 'I'm sorry about what happened back there - lousy husband of mine. Anytime you like it, drop in on me. Old Rubber Arm has got your voice pattern now. Ask for Cleopatra Jones. Only one thing - no more blue cats.'

III

I watched the pale-yellow circle of my lightbulb. It was all the illumination I could stand. Was I crazy? Was Zen a lunatic's dream cat? I totted up the evidence. Nobody but me had admitted to seeing Zen. And there were other indications of hallucination: the colour, the food, my fleeting hunch that Zen wasn't 'a cat.' Not to mention my godlike joy and sense of power. But those feelings of mine were the reason Zen *had* to exist. After what had happened, I couldn't endure life without Zen, without those insights that had shut away all sense of my lost job, my loneliness and my frustration. I fumbled in my pocket for the scribe tape Hercules Jones had given me.

Dr Womack.

Top of The Keep.

Eight O'clock.

I visualized the thin black shaft of The Keep, a luxurious office building, and the few minutes it would take me to get there. I crumpled the paper in my pocket and paced. Going to Dr Womack would mean I didn't believe in Zen.

I thought of the sleeping pills but was afraid there wasn't enough left. I reached for a book I'd been reading, but the idea of fiction was dull compared to what had happened. As a last resort, I turned on the tv.

'... freeing the murderous ravens of the antichrist.'

President McCarthy was warning his fellow countrymen about China all over again.

'There are sinners on this side of the Pacific battlegrounds,' the tremendous midwestern father-image continued, swaying forward and arching his bushy eyebrows. 'Sinners in our midst, creatures of the fleshpots. They have catered too long to the vilest desires and lusts.' he shook a finger and swayed once more. 'I warn them their time is at hand.'

 How could McCarthy make those futile and drunken threats when everyone knew his administration was hand in glove with Love Incorporated? I was about to change the channel but hesitated as an unfamiliar and eerie note crept into the President's voice.

'My fellow countrymen,' McCarthy whispered, wobbling a little from side to side. 'Strange forces are abroad, insane spirits of the upper air like those which troubled ancient Babylon. Our minds are being worked on; it is the final testing time for—'

My momentary curiosity gone, I returned the television to silence and darkness.

I must be crazy, I told myself with quiet certainty. Everything I'd done that afternoon had been out of character, including my ridiculous overvaluation of the dream cat.

Yes, I must be crazy.

A smaller and much brighter circle intersected the dim circle of my window. Celeste in the room across the way had switched on her light. Now she threw down her coat and walked around the room as if searching for something, the horsetail of black hair flirting from side to side. She turned her head this way and that. She was less than twenty feet away and wearing a grey suit adorned with great splotches of black. Her face was compact, nose small, mouth broad, eyes wide-set, and her ears had no lobes but curved to a faun-like tip. I felt a quiver of uneasiness.

As if giving up her hunt, she shrugged her shoulders and walked over to the window, looking straight at me. I shrank back a bit, though I was invisible to her. She grasped a dial on the window-sill and swung her hand in a quarter-circle, blacking the window out. As she turned away, the window brightened again until it was as transparent as before. I knew what must have happened. The inner pane of polarizing glass had missed its catch and revolved onward a few extra inches. I'd known it to happen to me.

Celeste thought she was hidden. She wasn't.

She stretched and took off her coat. I gnawed at my lip. Of course, I didn't want to watch her. But anything was welcome that would distract me from the miasma of failure with which my day was otherwise ending. She parted the magnetic clasps on her blouse and slipped out of it with a supple twist of her shoulders. She seemed to wear close-fitting, velvet black undergarments. She stepped out of her skirt. The undergarment ended at her thighs. It puzzled me because of the faint smokiness of the window. It looked as if it were a sort of fur. Balancing on one leg, she drew the stocking from the other, and along with the stocking, one of those grotesque ten-inch platform shoes. Only - and here my heart jumped - she seemed to have stripped off her foot. At the point where her ankle should have been, her leg curved backwards and forward again, slimming down to end in a neat little black hoof.

She stripped off the other stocking and shoe with the same result. The foot fitted into a well in the dummy foot and the platform. She turned on her radio and trotted around the room.

'Luck be a lady tonight.'

I heard the clicks of the little hoofs. saw her dainty fetlocks tufted with fur, the same texture and blackness as her 'undergarments.'

She stopped trotting, took an electric razor, and shaved the edge of her 'undergarment.'

'First a blue cat...' I mumbled.

I turned and plunged for the door. I wasn't clear about anything anymore. For instance, when I darted across the street two blocks away from the Skyway Towers, I was almost run down by a moving black electric car, designed in the antique, museum-case style of the early 2000s. Inside it was a monk and a nun, and a man named Virgil and a wrestler called Hercules with a box on his lap. I didn't even recognize them.

IV

The elevator whooshed to a stop. The door opened, and I stumbled out into a tiny foyer carpeted like a grey lawn. A wall - this one female - murmured, 'Good evening. Do you have an appointment?'

'Uh,' it surprised me I could speak at all.

'Do you have an appointment?' the wall repeated. 'Please answer yes or no.'

'Yes.'

'May I have your name, please?'

'Yes,'

'What is your name, please?'

'Maurice Tillet.' Soon, the words were out of my mouth, I wondered whether I shouldn't have said Hercules Jones, but the wall said, 'How do you do, Mr Tillet. Please come in.'

The wall slid open to reveal a pear-shaped room. A curved arm, slim and glittering as an eel, sprang out and showed me to a nearby chair with the gracious wave of a hostess who had studied ballet.

'Will you please sit?' the wall suggested. 'Dr Womack will be out in a shake of a lamb's tail.'

I took the suggestion. As if, by sinking into the chair, I had completed a circuit, the wall said, 'Thank you.'

I stood up.

The wall said, 'Yes?' with a hint of impatience. I sat again. 'Thank you,' the wall repeated.

The room was dark, soft, and silent as a womb. The inevitable desk had a double curve like a love seat. There were no adverts anywhere: a sure sign of wealth. On one wall was a large, round design, copied from a classical Greek original, which disturbed me with its nymph and satyr decoration. I shifted my gaze to an arch, through which I saw a stairway. Dr Womack must have had a penthouse upstairs.

I heard angry voices, male and female. The latter's rose to a cat squall of hate. A door shut with a snap, and a bit later, a man came down the stairs without moving his feet. I deduced an escalator.

Dr Womack had a few locks of dry white hair that clung to his scalp, like wildflowers fighting for life on a bare rock. He had a great moustache and four new, deep scratches on his left cheek, which he ignored and expected me to as well. We sat and looked at each other across the curved and gleaming desk.

'Well, Mr Tillet? Hercules told me you were coming, and since the monk and the nun are paying anyway, the new arrangement is fine.'

'Who are the monk and the nun?'

'The monk and the nun are friends of Hercules Jones'. I thought you might know them.'

'Should I?'

Dr Womack moustache rose and fell like seaweed on an ebbtide. 'You're an hour late for your appointment.'

A drop of blood fell from the deepest scratch onto his white shirt and spread.

'I was spending the time going crazy,' I said.

'You seem a bit wrought up.'

'A bit?'

'Well, Mr Tillet - may I call you Maurice? It is the rule rather than the exception these days. For a full twenty years now, the entire country has been living in an age of collective madness and herd delusion, comparable only to the Dutch tulip mania, the witch trials, or the dancing madness. I'm writing a book on it, you see. What other results could be expected when our society overvalues security, censorship, and the insatiable hunger for possessions?'

The analyst's moustache flexed as if there were a personal element in his anger

'Now, it may surprise you, but we won't be using any modern techniques such as electro sleep, deep brain photography or situational therapy. We shall do what our great-grandfathers would have done, talk. We can sit together yet need not look at each other. Now start at the beginning and tell me the story of your life.'

I swallowed.

'Excuse me, Dr Womack,' I said. 'But I'd rather not do that right now. I want to tell you about an experience, I mean, hallucination, I had that convinced me I'm crazy. I want you to interpret it or psych it or something.'

The analyst agreed. 'As good a beginning as any. Go ahead.'

So, I told him what I had seen through the quarter-darkened window. Under the analyst's expert rein-twitching, I admitted I had long used my window as an observation post. When I got to describing the hallucination itself, I trembled with restimulated terror, but I got it all out.

Dr Womack's moustache seemed delighted. As if I had presented him with a rare object of art. 'Beautiful!' he commented. 'I have seldom heard so magnificent a symbol for the murk longings of culture. A female satyr prepared to inflict both love and savage stampings,' he sighed. 'But, of course, I can't expect you to be interested in the artistic product of your unconscious creativity. You want to know about causes, sources. Tell me, have you ever seen a horse?'

'Once, in a zoo.'

'Any interest in Greek mythology?'

'None that I know.'

'Do you recall seeing the television program *Mr Ed; The talking horse?*'

'No.'

'Or the musical *The Horsy Set.*'

'*I can't say I have.*'

'Or the ancient, animated film, *Fantasia*?'

I shook my head. The analyst nodded.

'And the legs went straight down, like rods, to end in hoofs?'

'Not exactly,' I corrected and described the little heel bumps of the fetlocks and the slim pseudo-wrists of the pasterns.

'But otherwise, she was a normal girl? Except for the faun ears?'

'No,' I said. 'Her thighs were powerful as if made for galloping long distances. Her arms were sort of long. And they threw the upper part of her body forward a bit, if you know what I mean.'

'Magnificent!' the analyst crowed. 'Not only have you equipped your vision with exact horse-legs, but you have made compensations in the rest of the anatomy such as the mode of locomotion.'

He beamed under his moustache as if lost in admiration for the creative powers of the all-resourceful unconscious.

'Yes, but what does it say about my mind?' I would have been annoyed if I weren't so anxious. 'What's wrong with me?'

Dr Womack shook off my reverie with a smile.

'What's wrong with society?' he said. 'It's much too early for me to arrive at any conclusions or to help you arrive at your own. But, of course, the visual projection created by your unconscious has interesting references.'

'What are they?' I said. 'I may not have made it clear, but I'm worried about this. I can't get it out of my mind.'

Dr Womack smiled. 'A spot of interpreting would relieve you,' he agreed. 'Though you must remember it's an impromptu analysis and may be wrong. Here goes. The first thing that comes to mind is the dread of intimate experience and the instinct to invest it with terror. So, you feminize yourself by conceiving a hoofed love object, a trampling and punishing beast, self-punishment for your voyeurism. These fit in with the classical mythology about nymphs and their natural love companions, the goat-hoofed satyrs - the horse-hoofed centaurs, who were often, as you may remember, teachers of men.' The analyst frowned. 'It's possible you were projecting the wish to be taught about love. But...' he went on. 'I imagine the hidden significances are the more important ones. May I make a guess?'

I nodded as if my neck were afraid of the weight of my head.

'Are you a white-collar worker in close competition with robots?'

'Yes,'

The analyst's eyes beamed. 'In that case, we must suspect another mythological ingredient. Do you know the story of Pandora? Most people get the story wrong. There's a special point about it. Pandora was not an ordinary girl sent by the gods to bring humanity a box containing all ills. No, she was a metal maiden forged by Hephaestus at the command of Zeus. An automaton, a robot - bringing, in this case, the ills of the Second Industrial Revolution caused by introducing electronic calculators and senses.'

'But did Pandora have hoofs?'

Dr Womack waved away the objection. 'The unconscious is artistic about these things.'

'It is?'

'A visual projection, like a dream, can mean a thousand things. I warned you this was an impromptu analysis. We've carried it about as far as we can.'

'Look,' I said after a pause. 'There's a lot to the things you said, and some of them pushed buttons in my mind. But there's one thing still bothering me.'

'Go right ahead.'

'Is there any chance what I saw could be real? Any chance at all?'

The analyst chuckled. 'Not one in the world,' he said with complete conviction. 'If you knew half the things people tell me across this desk, normal neurotic people, I mean, you wouldn't worry so much. There's a woman, for instance, who keeps seeing shimmery moon-spiders in dark corners. There's a man who is always getting glimpses of a girl dressed in skin-tight mink, too. And there's another fellow who keeps waking in the middle of the night with the conviction he's in bed with - no, I shouldn't tell you that one.'

'But I could see it,' I persisted. 'It wasn't a glimpse of shadows.'

Dr Womack smiled. 'How many people have seen flying saucers? Including astronomers and atomic scientists. How many people have seen Elvis - walked and talked with him.? Besides all that, there were shadows! You said the polarizing window wasn't at its greatest transparency. You've been overdosing yourself with sleeping pills, and they can do funny things. For the hoofs, well, have you ever noticed high heels are like little hoofs? And the girl's hairdo, her suit splotched like a piebald horse, the remembered sound of the tap-dancing - don't you see your unconscious could weave those things?'

'I guess so,' I said. 'But there's one other thing. Something I saw this afternoon. I was with it for an hour. I touched it and fed it.'

'What other thing?' said the analyst, with the hint of an easy laugh.

'A blue cat.'

Dr Womack didn't answer. Instead, the four scratches and the dried trickles of blood on his left cheek stood out much more sharply as if he had grown pale.

'A blue cat?' His voice was a distant echo of itself.

'Yes.'

'Um,' the analyst sank farther down into his chair as if he were reaching for something with his toe.

Something beeped. The analyst snatched the phone. His face assumed a fierce expression, 'Yes ... no, I can't. I can't, I tell you. You couldn't; you'd get arrested. Well, but only for five minutes. Five minutes, do you hear? I'll be waiting.'

He replaced the phone and looked around at me with despair. His moustache twitched, and his enormous eyes turned comical.

'This is most embarrassing,' he said. 'A former patient insists on seeing me at once, threatens to cause a disturbance downstairs if I won't. She would, too. We had fine fracases before she broke off the analysis. I have no other course but to see her. I know how to appease her enough to get her home.'

'I'd better go,' I said, rising.

'I won't hear of it,' Dr Womack protested. 'I want to go much deeper into your case. The last thing you mentioned - it opened vistas! No, you wait for five minutes in the next room, ten at the most, and I'll have her out of here.'

'I'd rather go,' I said. 'If you don't mind.'

'Impossible,' Dr Womack pronounced, taking a firm hold of my arm. 'She's jealous of all my other patients and would be sure to attack you the instant you stepped out of the elevator. Did I tell you she carries a gold squirt gun filled with sulphuric acid? The only other way out is the service chute, and it's not designed for human use.'

He guided me through a door beyond the arch but not entering himself.

'You stay in here for five minutes. There's plenty to read and to glance over—not that you'll have much time. Trust me. Everything's under control.'

The door shut. One fleeting glance around showed shelves of books, racks of old magazines, a daybed, a central table, and a large mirror set in the ceiling. Despite the sober surroundings, I had no wish to stay in there a moment longer. I punched the door button. Nothing happened. I hit it again.

There hadn't been time for Dr Womack to have taken five steps away from the other side. I hammered on the wall.

'Dr Womack,' I called. 'Dr Womack!'

Then the lights went out.

V

The silence closed around me, like a preview of the mental hospital cell I suspected I would end up in. In the darkness, my heart pounded. After Dr Womack's casual acceptance of my satyr hallucination, I wondered why he should have tagged me a dangerous lunatic at the mere mention of a blue cat. Psychologists know things about the mind's secret language never told to ordinary people, I supposed. Innocent symbols could pick out murderers, traitors, and non-conformists that would otherwise slip by.

There was a sharp click. I looked up. A tiny line of light appeared on the ceiling, widened, and became an oblong spilling radiance on the table below. The mirror slid out of the way. No human figures were visible from where I stood, and I did not wish to step forward into the light. Was I so crazy the staff intended to fish for me with nets? A foot dangled over the edge.

It was a charming foot, slim and clad in the most shimmeringly expensive sort of stocking, which gave each toe its separate translucent compartment. Four black velvet straps ran back from between the toes, which helped attach an airy black shoe. The foot was followed by a second than by the rest of the girl. I got a quick impression of a short black evening dress, a black shoulder cape, long, dark hair cascading free and white arms in black gloves from above the elbows and ending at the knuckles.

She whirled on me like a black panther, complete even to the shrill snarl. The fingers of her right hand were tipped with clawed, silver thimbles, while in her left, she held ten gleaming inches of a knife, poised like a fencer, she waggled it under my chin.

'Did my father send you to spy on me?'

'No,' I said, not wanting my Adam's apple to protrude.

'Why are you in here, lurking in the dark?'

'Your father locked me in,'

'Is he doing it to his patients, too?' She lowered the knife to an easy, on guard position, which caused her cape to fall around her.

'He locked me in and turned off the lights,' I reaffirmed.

She slit her long-lashed eyes. 'He often sends his patients in here for observation.'

'Observation?'

She jerked a silver-fanged thumb at the ceiling.

'That mirror's transparent from above. He likes to watch what his patients do when they're alone.'

'If the mirror is transparent from above, why didn't you see me when he locked me in here?'

'Father always shuts the mirror off when he's not using it. He doesn't even know it can open.' She licked the centre of her upper lip with the tip of her tongue. 'You're likeable enough,' she said. 'Why did he lock you in here?'

'I mentioned a blue cat,' I said with a huffiness. 'He said something about my waiting here while he got rid of a violent ex-patient who carries around a...'

'Gold squirt gun? It is his pet dodge for getting rid of patients.'

'He doesn't want to get rid of me, does he?'

'No,' she said. 'He wants to keep you.'

'He wants to lock me in a mental hospital,' I said, hoping for her to disagree.

'I don't envy you,' she put the knife in a sheath in her skirt. 'Father favours old-fashioned treatments like convulsive therapy and simulated snake pits. Well, if the orderlies are on their way, I'd better be on mine.' She took three quick steps, looked back at me. 'Care to come with me? I always enjoy annoying my father.'

I lost no time saying, 'Yes.'

She headed for the back of the room.

'What's your name, by the way?'

'Judy,' she told me. 'Judy Womack.'

'Mine's Maurice,' I said. 'Maurice Tillet. Will you try for the elevator?'

'Of course not!' she snapped.

'But your father said the only other way is the....'

'Shh!' she hissed and punched a door button.

The wall kept blank. 'So, it's on code,' she said. 'I might have known.' She punched the button in a rapid rhythm. The wall was still blank. 'Oh, it's the special code, the one I'm not supposed to know.' She looked around at me. 'You must be important!' She punched the button in another rhythm. This time, to my surprise, the wall parted.

I followed her into a gleaming kitchen, complete with glassed-in shelves of gamma-sterilized yam steaks and carrots, freezer, TV oven, shadowed mushroom bed and small microbe tank for home-cultured appetizers. My eyes bugged at the latter two luxuries, but it occurred to me to say, 'What about the mirror you left open? Mightn't your father come in upstairs and see I've escaped?'

'We'll be gone by then.'

She was standing in front of a vertical cylinder half protruded from the wall and was busy once more with her button punching. A tiny blue light flashed up a tall column of studs like a skyrocket. A doorway about the size of a large cat opened in the cylinder.

'Get inside and squat in it. And squat straight, or you'll get your head rubbed off!'

'But this is the service chute, isn't it?' I said, withdrawing the foot I had inserted in the doorway,

'Did you expect Nubian slaves to carry you down in a chair? Get on with it.'

I got in, cracking the top of my head on the doorway, and drew in my legs and assumed the position of the Anxious Buddha.

'I'm sending you to the first basement,' she told me in clipped tones. 'I'll give you five seconds to get out. I'm pretty sure the door will be open.'

'You're pretty sure the door will be open?'

'Don't worry. I've done this a dozen times - or at least thought about doing it.'

My spine stiffened to condensed steel in the capsule, and my clenched hands became those of a gorilla. If only Zen were with me tucked inside my jacket.

The floor jerked down from under me, and my stomach scrambled over my heart and nestled below my tonsils. A giant snake hissed, and I was conscious of being inches from death by friction on every side. My heels cut into my rump, my vertebrae cut into my intervertebral disks, and various things inside me jarred loose.

Then, I was staring into an empty room. I dove out onto the floor, while behind me, the capsule took off with a hearty *whish*. By the time I had dragged myself to a sitting position and taken a few breaths, there was a gust of air from the chute and a *zing. Judy* sprang out and curtsied to an imaginary audience.

'You never did that before?'

'Of course, I have I, but I knew if I said I hadn't, you'd take it more seriously.' She tweaked me by the nearest ear. 'Come on. You're not out of my father's clutches yet.'

I scrambled to my feet and followed her.

'How did you push the button from the inside?'

'Taped it down, jumped in and shut the door.'

She led me into a shadowy garage, lined with ornate cars in stalls stacked like prison cells. Several of the vehicles had recharging cables plugged in. a ramp ahead led upward. Judy coded open the barrier in front of a small black car without a hint of decor.

'It's not my car,' she said as she hopped inside. 'I'm hiding it for friends.'

And with that far from reassuring remark, she guided the car out toward the ramp. A door rose at her voice. Then we were outside, speeding under amber streetlights.

We'd driven for a half-mile when a big car slammed to a stop in front of us. Two men jumped out of the car, bickering between themselves.

'Look, if this is another wild goose chase?' the first said in sceptical tones.

'Don't be absurd,' the other said in a voice I recognized as Dr Womack's. 'I tell you, he mentioned a blue cat.'

Suddenly, the analyst looked around and saw me gawking at him.

'There he is!'

Judy floored the small black car, and with the twang of hooked bumpers parting, we swung out into the street and away.

 I looked over my shoulder. 'They've got back in. They're turning around.'

'You must be important,' said Judy. 'Well, here goes,' and she nosed the car toward the narrow mouth of a ramp leading downward.

'Hey, that's 'Exit Only!"

'That's why I'm using it,'

I closed my eyes. The car tilted down, and the gods of probability appeared inclined to grant favours. So, I opened my eyes to the brighter, nearer, fog-lights of the under level as the car levelled out. Then, once more, I looked back.

'They've come after us,' I said.

'Very important,' Judy muttered, shaking her head. 'Prepare for acceleration and hope they stacked the cars right at the next ten intersections.'

There was a red glow behind us as the pursuing car shrank in size. Twisting around with difficulty, the fog lights had become a molten yellow ribbon. The car flew past the hood of a truck entering from a side street, though our speed made it appear to be standing still. Blocks ahead, we shot between two cars, which seemed frozen. The red glow died. We sailed up to another 'Exit Only' ramp into the spectral yellow night. Proceeding at speed soon became reasonable, and we turned four successive corners.

'That should do it,' Judy said with professional nonchalance. 'Ralf put in the rockets yesterday. I wasn't altogether sure he had them lined upright. A neat little trick, isn't it?'

'I guess,' I assured her with a shiver.

'I kind of like you. You're so darn scared and innocent, yet you play along. I'm sure I can persuade Ralf to let you join the gang.'

Neither Judy Womack's criminal pastimes nor her friendliness could hold my attention. Staring out at the jaundiced street, I was thinking of Zen and of the way I felt when Zen was with me.

'What is this blue cat, anyway?' said Judy. 'A carved emerald or a password to a secret society?'

'It's a cat.'

'Fine,' she said. 'Don't tell me!'

She speeded up again and ran through a stoplight that protested after her. Her eyes gleamed in their circles of black liner.

'Ralf has a bunch of sales robots lined up. We can ram them and grab them, one, two, three!'

I felt like I was waking from a dream. 'Well, that's kind of you!' I said. 'But if you could drop me home, it'd be great. 3765 Alta Brea Crescent.'

She looked at me with surprise.

'All right,' she said after a bit, 'I'll do it, if only because I got such a kick out of the look on your face when you got in the chute.'

She spun the car in a tight U-turn. We sped for a while in silence. I became aware Judy was stealing glances at me.

'If you cook up a little nerve and change your mind,' she growled. 'You might find us at the Tan Jet much later tonight.'

I didn't comment. She went on.

'Night's the only time, you know, at least in this century - night in the city. I love the pale-yellow streets and the bright yellow tunnels. They've taken the jungles away from us, the high seas, highways, even space and the air. They've cancelled half of the night. They've tried to steal danger. But we've found it again in the city; we who've got the nerve! Well, here's your 3765 Alta Brea Crescent,' she said, jerking the car to a stop. 'Seems like a pleasant neighbourhood to have bad habits in.'

I opened the door.

'Are you sure you don't want to join me, Maurice?' she said.

I turned to shut the door.

'Thanks, but I've had enough excitement for one day.'

VI

I took the elevator up to my level. I went along the corridor to the tune of a muted radio behind a door. I needed a drink, life insurance, a holiday, and a home in the provinces. I didn't switch the light on inside the door. Instead, I made straight for the kitchenette but stopped short by three or four feet. Something was wrong - something in the air, a scent. I stood still and listened. The smell in the air was a perfume, a heavy, cloying perfume. There was no sound, no sound at all. My eyes adjusted to the darkness, and I groped for the wall switch with my thumb and flicked the light on. A tall figure came out of the bathroom, dressed in an aggressive dowdiness: long shapeless frock, button shoes, and a wide-brimmed hat.

'Cleopatra? How did you get in?'

'I came through the keyhole, like Tinkerbelle.'

'What do you want?'

'No more questions,' she said, grabbing my elbow. 'Come with me.'

The next moment, she was carrying me down the hallway. I expected her to stop soon as we got out of sight of the room, but she carried on down the stairs and out into the street.

'Look here Mister!'

'Maurice.'

'Well, Maurice, can I take you to dinner?'

'Do I have a choice?'

'No,' she said. She kept peering about and didn't slacken the pace. 'I know a good soy place. It's quiet, and they know how to broil a good yam.'

It was raining outside, hot rain that curls your hair and makes your nerves jump and your skin itch. Far off, the banshee wail of police or fire sirens rose and fell, never completely silent. Cleopatra carried me into a narrow, shadowy side street and finally put me down. A little door led into a long dark room with a counter along one side and a row of booths along with the other. With its chrome finishes, it had to date back to 1960. The customers were big men, divided between chauffeurs, security guards, and a less definable category. There was an elevator door next to the one we'd come in from. Cleopatra wagged her big hand at a couple of servers.

'Whiskey and yams, and make sure you burn the edges. What'll you have, Maurice?'

I hadn't eaten in a long time and mumbled something about wanting a yeast sandwich and a glass of soybean milk. Cleopatra passed on my order without comment and took me in tow once more. She had to answer a few familiar greetings.

'No autographs tonight, my dears. Even wrestlers are entitled to a night off!'

Still, she spent little time on them and seemed relieved when she plunked me down in the booth nearest the front door. There the rumble of trucks was loudest, and their headlights flashed on the scratched and dusty plastic. I studied my companion across the table and traced a recent bruise on her enormous jaw, half-concealed by makeup. She dove into her pocketbook with a fluster and dabbed at her jaw with a powder puff but gave up, put it back and slumped forward on the plastic.

'Never let them tell you wrestling matches are fixed,' she said. 'Hercules bust a gut trying to beat me tonight.'

'You won?'

'You better believe I won. Two falls, a spaceship spin, and a free-fall - when I throw them out, they don't come back.'

A tray came sliding along the bar. Cleopatra went and got it before I realised it was for us. Cleopatra's seared yams were big - while her whiskey was vast and brown. I nibbled my yeast sandwich and found it okay, though it always made me uneasy eating food that didn't pop out of a wall.

As Cleopatra munched her yams and drank her whiskey, she told me a snatch of the story of her life. It turned out she was a farm girl who had come to the city young and suffered the usual disillusionments.

'How's a girl going to get ahead these days?' she said. 'I was too big and strong. I scared the men. So, I tried out scrub mothering for a while - you know, birthing babies for wealthy women who didn't want to carry them the nine months themselves - but there was no future in it. I remembered I could pin nine out of ten boys back home, so I entered amateur wrestling contests and pretty soon, they were grooming me for a pro.' She shook her head. 'You should have seen my figure; it was beautiful before they put me on hormones.'

She inspected her enormous hands, still white-gloved though now gravy stained. 'Even used pituitrin on me.' She sighed. By now, she had reduced her yams to air and was working on her second whiskey. 'So that's the way it was. Of course, I had to fall in love with a wrestler and marry him - most of the girls in the business make the same mistake.'

 'Well, at least you got a job with security.'

'Are you kidding? Male-female wrestling is done for. The government's going to issue a crackdown.'

'They always say that, and it never happens.'

'This time, it will.'

'I heard the president talking about something tonight,' I said. 'But Love Incorporated has so many connections with the government,'

'You're right. The best connections any syndicate ever had. But this time, they're finished. Mr Treacle has been worried for weeks.'

'Mr Treacle? '

She lifted her heavy eyebrows. 'Don't you know Mr Treacle?'

I shook my head.

'You saw him for a minute this afternoon.'

I did?' I got a foggy memory flash of a door-filling hulk with sunglasses.

'Mr Treacle is on top of the syndicate, just underneath Mr Brimstone himself!'

I didn't recognize the second name either and Cleopatra quit trying. 'Well,' she said. 'There's Mr Treacle, the boss of Love Incorporated, which runs wrestling and amusement centres, all sales robots, jukebox burlesque, and a lot of other things they don't talk about. He's worried, and I know he doesn't worry about anything but the syndicate. So, things must be terrible.' She paused and added, 'Lots of things are terrible.'

I nodded.

'Say,' she said, watching her big, gravy-stained finger rub her near-empty glass. 'Was that a hallucination you had this afternoon? When were you talking about a blue cat?'

'I'm not sure.'

She let out an enormous sigh.

'If there is a cat, it could be worth $10,000?'

'$10,000? What made you think of that figure?'

'Well,' she said. 'After you left this afternoon, Hercules started talking about how dumb I was. Only this time, it wasn't because I had let you in, but because I'd let you go. He says to me, 'Cleo, you don't recognize the opportunity I had to make $10,000.' I didn't overthink about it at the time because he's always trying to needle me. But after I got out of the ring tonight, Mr Treacle asked me about a blue cat. '

'What did you say?'

'I told him you were a harmless nut.'

'You told him I'm a nut?'

'Didn't you think you were a nut this afternoon? You didn't believe in a blue cat after we'd argued you out of it!'

'I changed my mind after I went to see the analyst.'

I sketched the essentials of my episode with Dr Womack. Cleopatra looked concerned.

'If he locks you up and calls in the hoods, that blue cat is no dream!'

'His daughter didn't think the blue cat was important.'

'Judy? You can't trust her!'

I hadn't realised I'd told her so much about Judy.

'Besides,' Cleopatra went on, 'Mr Treacle must be interested in the blue cat, or he wouldn't ask me about it, and anything Mr Treacle is interested in has got to be real.'

'What are you talking about?'

Cleopatra's brow furrowed. 'This is the way I figure it: Mr Treacle told Hercules he was going to pay $10,000 to anybody who brought him a blue cat.'

'But why would Mr Treacle want a blue cat? Did you ask him?'

'You don't ask Mr Treacle anything,'

'So, your husband stole the blue cat while Old Rubber Arms was keeping me out?'

Cleopatra's look implied I stated the obvious far too often.

'Where is Hercules now?'

'Most likely, gone off with Virgil.'

'But if your guess is right about Mr Treacle offering $10,000 for a blue cat, and Hercules stole the cat, why hasn't he taken it to him?'

'Get one thing straight,' she said. 'I love Hercules. I've taken a lot from him, but I haven't minded too much. Oh, it hurt when I found out he thought more of Virgil than he did for me, but I didn't let it under my skin. After all, if a man knows you can pin him in a wrestling match, it's bound to affect him.'

She took the glass out of her hand and made claws.

'If I had the little rat here, I'd strangle some sense into him. But until Mr Treacle talked to me, I suspected nothing was wrong, and now I can't do anything about it.'

A blurred memory became clear. I told Cleopatra about racing to Dr Womack's. How I had seen Hercules, and Virgil, driving somewhere in an old electric car.

'With a monk and a nun,' I said.

Cleopatra gave me a look that ought to have stuck at least four inches out of my back. 'I should have known it.' She slammed the table with both fists, jumped up and grabbed me by the wrist. She fumbled for her glass, got mine instead, and recognized it before draining the last of the soybean milk. She set it down with a shudder and yanked me out of the booth.

'Come on,' she said.

'Where are we going?'

'We're going to the temple!'

VII

Cleopatra had been silent during most of the cab ride as if the whiskey had gone sour inside her, and when I made a move to pay, she motioned me aside. I hopped out, eager to see what the temple looked like, as if my hopes and fears had rotated again when the wheels of the cab stopped. Cleopatra's reference to 'the temple' had led me to expect Greek columns or an Egyptian portal. Instead, I was facing an oblong of darkness, framed by the sidewalk. I crossed the sidewalk and hesitated as if I stood on the edge of nothingness. Before me, a house took shape - an old, three-story place, with slanting roofs and lights gleaming through shuttered bay windows and fanciful dusty lights. Something gritted under my foot, and I noticed a yard of dirt between me and the house. It must have been the ground level of the city a hundred years ago. The windows peered across the gap far above my head. The house was so ancient and rickety it needed props.

But a new situation presented itself. The house was in the city's heart, hemmed in by gigantic buildings on every side. There should have been tiers of lighted windows and, far overhead, a square of the night sky. Instead, there was only darkness as if the pre-atomic age house existed in a private night. Headlights of turning cars in the street two levels above swept across the upper third of the house. All around were surfaces painted a dull, non-reflecting black.

'Legal business,' Cleopatra said, coming up beside me. 'Hercules told me something about it. The original owners couldn't be bought out, but the city seized the air-rights and built over them.'

I followed her across the yard to the rickety steps leading to the porch. My hand groped for a rail and touched peeling old paint.

Halfway up, a cat darted past me.

I swallowed my heart. The cat paused at the top. It was sprinkled with dark and light shades of blue - Zen. It loped around a corner of the porch. Following it, Cleopatra and I faced a six-panelled door lit by a dingy globe, which I guessed must be an ancient tungsten-filament lamp. There was no sign of the cat, but a tiny swinging door cut in the bottom of the big one.

Ignoring a cat-headed knocker, Cleopatra pounded on the door in a way that made me hunch my shoulders and keep an apprehensive eye on the ceiling. But the house didn't collapse. After a time, a peephole opened above the knocker, and a watery grey eye surveyed them.

'I want to see that no-good husband of mine,' said Cleopatra. It didn't sound like her usual self-confident roar.

'Now Cleo, you're all upset,' came the reply. 'Your aura's all muddy; I can't see you through it.'

'Listen here, you let me in, or I'll bust your lousy temple down.'

This was not a threat to be taken lightly, but it didn't faze the voice owner.

'No, Cleo,' he said. 'I can't let you in when your vibrations are like that. Later - we may even help you achieve inward tranquillity - but not now.'

'Look,' said Cleo. 'I got a friend with me who's got business with you.'

'What business?'

I looked straight at the eye and said, 'The blue cat.'

The door swung back, and the owner of the voice appeared. The monk was wearing an orange beret and pants with a robe of bronze embroidered blue. He waved me in with an arm clad in emerald silk.

'All doors must open to him who speaks his name,' he said. 'Do you vouch for your companion's peacefulness?'

'I wouldn't touch anybody or anything here,' Cleopatra growled.

'From filth, the roses spring, Cleo,' the monk reminded her. 'And good blooms from evil. Be happy you are to share in the great transformation.'

I stood on the threshold of a large living room twisting with streams of incense and cluttered with Victorian furniture and bric-à-brac of ornaments and objects suggesting every religion in the world. The lights here, too, were tungsten and too few to make many shadows. At the far end of the room was a large doorway curtained with black velvet. Through the resinous odour of incense came the dull reek of stale food, clothes, and people, a sour animal smell.

The room was alive with cats: black, white, topaz, silver, taupe; striped, mottled, banded, pied; short-haired, Angora, Persian, Siamese, and Siamese mutant. They dripped from chair tops and shelves; they peered from under little tables and from crevices between cushions. One stretched full length on the woven buddha in the centre of a prayer rug; another lay on a tarnished silver pentacle inlaid in a dark, low table. One was battling a phylactery hanging from the wall, making the little leather box swing and jump; another was nosing a small steatopygia figurine; yet another was entangling itself in a rosary; two were lapping dirty looking milk from a silver chalice set with amethysts.

And in the centre of a mantlepiece over a real fireplace, and midway between a gilded icon and a tin Mexican devil-mask, there posed most sublimely still of all, with forelegs straight as spears ... the blue cat.

As I walked forward, I heard the monk say.

'That is not his true self, but his simulacrum, his ancient Egyptian harbinger.'

I came closer. It indeed was the bronze statue of a cat, with the hue of Zen's coat. Coming up beside me, the monk explained, 'As soon he came, I routed out all our relics. Most of them are in there,' he showed me the black velvet curtains. 'But a few are here.'

Besides the bronze statue, the monk pointed out a small mummy case and inside it the linen-banded mummy of a cat, looking like a sack with a blob at the top. The monk was explaining the tiny Canopic jar of preserved cat entrails beside it. A six-toed Siamese wandered up and sniffed the mummy.

I found my voice. 'Do you have Zen?'

The monk's high curved eyebrows curved still higher. 'Zen?'

'The blue cat,' I added.

The monk's face grew grave. 'No one has the blue cat. It has us. We are his humble worshippers, his primal hierophants.'

'I want to see him.'

'All in good time,' The monk assured me. 'When he wakes, and the world changes. Meanwhile, compose yourself.'

'Why is this blue cat so important, anyway? What is it?'

The two men turned. Cleopatra was still standing on the threshold. She swayed forward a little, hugging her elbows, yet had her shoulders squared, and she was glaring at them, like a very tall rebellious schoolgirl.

'The blue cat is love,' The monk said. 'The love that blossoms even from hate.'

There was another interruption. This one took the form of a coy, girlish snicker. I turned to the side of the room I had not yet inspected, the one facing the fireplace. A wide bay window shuttered with grey jalousies were all the other windows in the room except for one fronting on darkness beside the fireplace. The bay was a semi-circular couch on which a nun sprawled, still in a black sweater and stiff, red skirt.

'I can't get used to the idea of loving everything,' she said. 'The monk says I've got to be nice to people and stop sticking pins in them, but it's hard.'

For a morbid moment, I thought she was referring to the cats. I saw a series of narrow shelves behind her, at the top of the couch and going halfway up the bay. They were crowded with dolls. Not ordinary dolls but realistic human figures, most of them about six inches high. There must have been two or three hundred. They lined up behind the nun, like the cross-section of a three-level house in some tiny living world. In front of the couch was a low table crowded with wax blocks, moulds, micro-tools, and magnifiers. Several completed figurines and piled squares of fabrics so delicate they must have been woven especially.

'You like my little people? They like having pins stuck through them.'

The dolls represented actual individual people-perfect statuettes of the rich and famous. I recognized President McCarthy, China's Lin Xi, square-jawed J. Robert Oppenheimer of the Federal Bureau of Investigation, several TV stars, the monk, about eight versions of the nun herself, Hercules Jones in black tights, Cleopatra in maroon ones, Dr Womack and Judy Womack in an evening dress much like the one I'd seen her wearing.

'Recognizing friends?'

Footsteps clumped. Cleopatra stood behind me, looking at the dolls. The nun looked up at her with an innocent smile. 'They're adorable, aren't they?'

'Ugh!' said Cleopatra.

'Try to be joyful,' The monk admonished with a wag of his finger. 'It will be much easier when he wakes. I must see if there has been any change. Amuse yourselves, won't you?'

Having set them a stupendous task, the monk hurried from the room, his blue robes whistling against the black velvet curtains.

'The monk's been as efficient as can be ever since he came,' The nun observed. 'I've never seen him so peppy before about anything. Ever since Hercules handed him the blue cat, all cute and curled-up and sleeping.'

'It wasn't sleeping,' I cut in. 'A stun-gun had knocked him out.'

'Don't be ridiculous,' The nun went on. 'Hercules found him sleeping. The monk touched him. He told us the world would change, and there would be a new era of love and understanding, and ever since then, he's been busy a little bee. Soon as we got home. He whirled around and got out all the Bastet icons. I told the monk because Bastet was a lady goddess, maybe we shouldn't call him *he*. But the monk told me no, that was it. And I guess maybe he's right, because when the monk carried him through here sleeping, all the little cats went for him in a big way, and the little girl cats went for him even more than the little boy cats. I always trust the monk's notions because he's so good at ESP and telepathizing. I make half our living by it.'

There was a strangled grunt, and I heard the clumping again behind me. The nun smiled and followed Cleopatra with her eyes but kept on babbling.

'I guess there is something to what the monk says about an era of love because these little cats used to fight all the time, but ever since *he's* been in the house, they've been peaceful as anything - a regular little cat UN without China and the satellites. Even I'm sweeter, though it's going to break my heart not to hate people,' she sighed. 'Still, if everybody's going to have to love people, I'll have to practice.'

She reached behind her and took down the doll of Cleopatra. 'I should even love *her*,' she said.

The footsteps changed direction and came stamping through the curtain. Cleopatra's face was brick red from rage.

'You put me down!' she said. 'Only witches make wax dolls of people and stick pins in them.'

By way of reply, the nun gave the figurine an affectionate stroke.

'No, Cleopatra, I'm going to have to love you, and you're going to have to get used to it. If I had any choice, I would much rather stick needles through you.'

Cleopatra writhed at every touch the nun gave the figurine.

'Put me down!' she bellowed, raising her arms with all the muscles standing out underneath her dress's long, tight sleeves.

The nun complied without haste and took down another of the figurines. Her voice was soft, like a serpent gliding. 'Would you mind if I practised loving on Hercules?'

'Don't you touch him either!' Cleopatra's face was purple. 'It's bad enough you're going all gooey over him in the flesh. Stop touching him that way!'

Cleopatra kicked the worktable to one side, so its contents scattered, and all the cats went scampering under tables and chairs. 'I'm going to smash every one of those dolls,' she announced, advancing.

The nun rose to her knees on the couch, her back to her little people, her arms outstretched to either side.

'Straight through the eyes,' she hissed, her face a fury's mask. "That's where *your* needles are going!'

There was frantic padding of feet on the stairs, and Hercules Jones and Virgil burst into the room from the hall.

'Cleo!' yelled Hercules. 'I told you I'd kill you if you ever came here!'

'He will, too,' Virgil confirmed.

Cleopatra turned on Hercules, assuming the stance of a bear.

'Listen, you ten-timing little arse. You're going straight home with me.' She hitched up her skirt and rolled up the long sleeves of her dress.

Meanwhile, Hercules was surveying the scene and getting an exact idea of how much damage was done.

'Cleo,' he said, shocked but advancing, 'Don't you know what you've done?' Hercules continued with aggrieved anger to convince Cleopatra of the enormity of her actions. 'You've done the one thing I won't ever forgive.' he was tearful. 'Don't you know the monk and the nun are the only two people in the world who mean anything to me?'

The retort came not from Cleopatra but Virgil.

'Oh, so you care nothing about me, either?'

'Shut up, you're a dumb stooge,' Hercules told him without looking around.

'Oh, so I'm a dumb stooge, am I? Well, let me tell you, Hercules, Cleo's right about one thing. These religious types have turned your head. They've dazzled you.'

The monk came popping back into the room. his brilliant silk robes hissing against the black velvet. 'Stop, at once!' he commanded, raising his arm. 'You will disturb his awakening.'

'Shut up,' Virgil snarled. 'I don't want to hear any more about your stupid cult. Could we have got *ten thousand dollars* for that cat? We were all ready to hand it over to Mr Treacle when you had to prance in with *that ugly* witch of yours and flatter Hercules into thinking he was starting a new religion.'

He stepped toward the monk, puffing out his chest like a bright blue fighting cock.

But the monk's horrified and reproachful gaze turned not on Virgil but Hercules.

'Hercules,' he gasped. 'Do you mean to tell me you dreamed of selling *him* for money?'

'Now see what you've done,' Hercules moaned at Cleopatra. 'You've spoiled everything.'

'I'll spoil you,' she roared and ran at him like a bull. Hercules stepped to one side and slipped out a hand for a hold. But Cleo's professional training came back to her. she checked herself, grabbed the wrist of the hand snaking toward her, bent, spun, and sent Hercules sailing over her hip, landing him on the silver pentacle table. It toppled with a crash, and various religious objects fell from the wall.

Meanwhile, the nun picked up a small vase that had broken from her upset worktable and hurled it at Virgil's head. Virgil chucked himself at the monk's throat, and the vase passed through space where Virgil's head had been. While all this was going on, I stepped over to the shelves of figurines, picked up Judy, and put her in my jacket pocket.

Hercules selected a black glass Aztec sacrificial knife from the fallen religious objects and writhed to his knees like a cobra. Cleopatra picked up a tiny but excellent brass Buddha. Nearer the velvet curtains, Virgil had the monk on his back and was choking him, while the monk tried to beat Virgil on the head with the silver chalice from which the cats had been drinking. The nun grabbed a fistful of hatpins and darted forward to Virgil.

Not even in the trenches and foxholes had I seen actual murder in a human face.

Now I saw it in five.

And then suddenly it wasn't there at all.

The room grew still. The black glass knife and the chalice clattered from Hercules's and the monk's hands. The nun's hatpins struck the floor with a faint, vibrant rattle. Cleopatra's Buddha thudded on the prayer rug. Virgil's hands unlocked even before they had a message from his brain. Expressions unlocked too. Hateful furrows softened and vanished. Lips writhed back from teeth and returned eyes filled with painful longing.

Hercules said in a soft, fantastic voice.

'Cleo, I love you.'

Cleopatra said, 'You care what I think, don't you, Hercules?!'

Virgil said to the monk, 'You're not a fraud after all.'

The nun said, 'You want Hercules to be happy, Virgil. It isn't vanity and envy.'

The monk said, 'Oh my God, it's happening.'

My feelings were in that golden sea they'd swum in before. As if sensitive strands joined my heart to those of the five persons around me. It even seemed to me there were delicate, gossamer wires connecting me to the nun's figurines. For that moment, I understood Womack, McCarthy, Lin Xi, and maybe even myself.

I turned toward the velvet curtains. A few inches above the floor, Zen's little blue head poked through. It hung there like a blue jewel, flooding us with its mellow rays. It pushed through the curtains and, from under tables and chairs, the fireplace. From behind tiers of books, all the other cats appeared and gathered around Zen in a circle.

'It has happened,' The monk whispered. 'The world is changing.'

'A living god,' The nun murmured. 'Incarnate in a cat.'

Zen strolled across the room. The other cats made way for him and followed him, keeping a respectful distance. He passed the nun and Virgil and the monk, who looked a shade disappointed and sprang into my arms.

I had held nothing that weighed so little or felt so electric. My chest seemed to be too small for my heart.

The monk called out, 'You are the chosen one.'

I looked at him and, with an unreasoning and mystical gust of apprehension, at the black window behind him. The glass in the window was vibrating. Circular grey waves were spreading from a central spot. At the same instant, I felt my left hand, the one cradling Zen, go numb. Zen leapt in the air and fell six feet away from me. The glass in the window shattered all at once and tinkled to the floor, leaving only a few jagged shards around the frame. Zen's cat parade broke up, and its members raced into the hall and up the stairs.

Mr Treacle leapt in through the window, with a suppleness one would never have expected of his vast body. He stood inside, gripping a stun-gun in his big mitt.

'There's a couple of boys with guns out there,' said Mr Treacle, stepping to one side of the window. 'You don't want to get yourselves shot up.'

Nobody did.

'Listen, everybody,' he said. 'So long as you forget about all this, so long as you act like it never happened, I'm going to forget all about you. That goes for you too, Hercules, and for you, Cleo, and Virgil, if I get the littlest hint, you've remembered...' he scanned their faces. 'Okay,' he said, shifting the gun to his left hand. He stepped forward and scooped up Zen.

'He ... he ...' The monk stuttered. Mr Treacle looked at him, and the monk fell quiet.

'How long did this cat sleep after you stun-gunned it?'

'Until now,' said Hercules.

Mr Treacle backed away toward the window. I felt something turning inside me. Something was spurring me into movement. I advanced toward Mr Treacle, a shaky step, then a couple more, all the while fearing imaginary bullets racking my torso.

'Put the cat down,' I croaked.

'He's a nut,' said Hercules. 'He won't cause trouble.'

'I can see that,' Mr Treacle said, shifting the gun to the hand from which Zen dangled. But I kept on toward the towering figure. I tried to stop, but my body wouldn't let me - and now, once again, the same internal torturer pried open my teeth and lips.

'Put him down. You can't have him. Nobody can.' I raised my fists.

Mr Treacle's enormous fist came toward my jaw in slow motion. Still, there wasn't enough time to get out of the way.

VIII

You can have a hangover from other things than alcohol. I had one from a punch in the face. My head seemed twice as thick as usual to me, but I didn't feel any pain until my exploring hands came to the lump on my chin.

'You're okay,' said Cleopatra. I doubted it. I swivelled my head around. The nun was busy at her worktable. The monk was in conference with Hercules and Virgil.

'He's a what?' said Virgil.

'A Satanist, a devil-worshipper,' said the monk. 'It would explain him stealing the blue one. Plus, he is called Mr Treacle. There is a clue in the name.'

'Stop talking,' said Virgil. 'Mr Treacle isn't interested in anything except money. Neither is Mr Brimstone. And Mr Treacle wouldn't be working for anyone but Mr Brimstone. Isn't that right, Hercules?'

Hercules wasn't talkative, but he did nod his head in agreement.

Cleo put a glass in my hand.

'Here, drink this,' she said.

'What is it?'

'Not soybean milk. Drink up!'

The whiskey, which tasted as if they laced it with something bitter, burned my throat and brought tears to my eyes. But at once, my head felt better. I surveyed the room. They had cleaned none of the mess up other than the nun's worktable.

'And your idea about the cat being mystical is rubbish too,' said Virgil.

The monk looked at him and Hercules with exquisite blankness. 'Didn't you feel it?' Didn't you feel what it did to all of us?'

Hercules shifted but didn't meet my gaze. 'We were all worked up, between your mumbo-jumbo and the fighting,' he said. 'We'd have believed anything.'

'But didn't you feel your whole being change?' said the monk. 'Didn't you feel universal love and understanding?'

'I didn't feel a thing.!' said Virgil. 'Did you, Hercules?'

Hercules didn't nod his head, but he didn't shake it either. And he didn't look at the monk.

The latter surveyed them both with sad resignation. 'You've forgotten,' he said. 'You've made yourselves forget. But how do you explain the behaviour of the cats? They recognized the Blue One. They tendered his worship.'

'They panted around after him,' Virgil said. 'He's an oversexed mutant. And another thing - if the cat's mystical and all dripping with powers, why was he knocked out? Why wasn't Mr Treacle all overcome with peace and love?'

'There was glass and distance between them,' said the monk.

'Then how did Hercules knock him out in the first place?'

'I stunned him,' said Hercules. 'I glimpsed something out of the corner of my eye and shot. I thought it was a mouse.'

'Whether you meant to or not, you stun-gunned it,' said the monk. 'I suppose the blue one was taken by surprise. Even gods have limitations.'

Virgil made a rude noise.

The monk grinned a gloriously warm grin, like the kiss of death.

 'Well, if I have to descend to your materialistic level, what is it makes the Blue One so important to Mr Treacle?'

'How should I know?' said Virgil. 'Maybe he's smuggling secrets for China!'

'Well ...,' said the monk.

I got to my feet and squared my shoulders.

'We can rescue him,' I said. 'We can rescue the blue cat. Who's with me?'

'No one,' said Virgil.

Cleo heaved herself out of her chair and lumbered over with her glass and bottle. 'Look,' she said, 'I got to admit you're a spunky little mutt. But nobody, nobody, goes up against Mr Treacle.'

'I did,' I said.

'Yeah, but it didn't go well.'

I looked at the monk. 'How about you? You believe in Zen?'

Virgil glared at the monk.

'If any of us bothers Mr Treacle about the blue cat, we'll all be inhaling bullets!'

The monk was looking around for advice. Finally, his gaze settled on the nun.

'What should we do?'

'I don't care what anyone else does,' she said. 'I'm working on Mr Treacle in my little way.'

She held up a small wax head that looked like the assistant boss of Love Incorporated.

'Ugh!' said Cleopatra.

The monk gnawed his lip and, with a wary eye on Hercules and Virgil, said, 'Yes, I suppose that's the best way after all.'

I headed for the door.

'Where are you going?' said Virgil.

'I'm going to get my cat back,'

There was a rush of competing voices, assuring me I would do no such something, but it was Cleopatra who grabbed my shoulders and swivelled me around.

'You can do nothing about that cat. You've got to get that through your head once and for all.'

I smiled at her. She shook her head.

'I shouldn't have given you whiskey.'

'It wasn't the whiskey, but what you put in it,' Virgil said. 'He's high as a kite.'

I grinned at him as if to prove his point. They all stepped back a bit and recognized my supreme self-confidence and bowed to the inevitable.

Dr Womack put down a black bag inside the doorway and stepped forward,

 'Hello all,' he said before turning his gaze to me. 'Well, that was quite a chase you led me on. I am fortunate to have found you at all. It was a most interesting conversation we were having, and I'm eager to continue it.'

He spared the others a glance. 'You'll excuse us talking professional matters, I hope. Now, I imagine the person who persuaded you to run away tried to put many ideas into your head. But I'm sure I can show you how nonsensical they are. It was the same person who turned out the lights in the first place and put all the doors on code. All that, and she's my daughter, too!'

'What do you want?'

'I want you to say goodbye to your friends. I hope they won't be too angry with me for dragging you away.'

Dr Womack was far enough into the light I could see the four streaks of dried blood on his cheek.

'I never believed in that wild woman patient of yours who was always threatening mayhem,' said the nun. 'But somebody clawed your face pretty good.'

Dr Womack's smile thinned a trifle.

'A few illusions turn out to be real. Like young women with hoofs and black fur, Maurice?'

'Or blue cats, Dr Womack?' I said. 'By the way, these people here have all seen the blue cat.'

'I didn't,' said Virgil.

'I don't know what that nut is talking about,' Hercules insisted. 'I'd always thought him half-baked, but now I suspect they didn't even put him in the oven. We'll be glad to get rid of him.'

Cleopatra looked like a bulldog that had just been kicked in the ribs and had its dinner sneaked by the cat.

'I don't like the idea of tossing the little guy to the wolves,' she said.

'To the wolves, Cleopatra? Please explain!'

The monk came hustling forward with great determination. 'Hercules is right,' he announced, seizing me by the shoulder and marching me toward the door. 'I'm tired of your deceptions, Mr Tillet.'

There was a grunt of satisfaction from Dr Womack. I tried to twist away from the monk, but the latter pressed even more closely to my side, so my face was next to his ear, and whispered, 'Up the stairs, two flights.'

I pushed away while the monk reeled with a yelp into Dr Womack, who was stooping for his black bag. I was racing up the creaking stairs in the darkness, while behind me were shouts and racing footsteps. Nearest were those of the monk, who was crying, 'There he goes! After him, everyone!'

I raced along the backstretch of the corridor and up the second flight, the monk flapping at my heels. At the top, he grabbed me and shoved me through a door.

'Out the window and over the beam,' he whispered.

The door shut, and the monk yelled, 'He's gone up in the attic. Follow me.'

I was in darkness, facing a tall window illuminated from the outside. About my feet, cats who had taken refuge in the room hurried. I crept over to the ancient double-paned glass. I considered the impossibility of opening such primitive windows, but one came up enough and all the way. I ducked through and crouched on the sill outside, steadying myself with one hand. Around me was nineteenth-century, musty smelling wood and slate. Opposite me, about twenty feet away, was the top-level street, busy with speeding cars. A metal beam about eight inches wide was Joining the two, outlined in the glow from the car's headlights. The shaft was grimy with dirt and based in the brick chimney beside the window. One of my feet was on it. Below were two stories of darkness.

What happened next may well have been possible because of the fear-abolishing, nerve-steadying drug Cleopatra had put in my whiskey. But I laid it to the influence of Zen and the monk's bizarre yet thrilling injunction. Indeed, I was no athlete. At any rate, I got to my feet, let go of the window, poised myself, and ran across the beam. I rolled over the railing at the other end and sprawled on the sidewalk. At the same instant, a needle of glaring blue lanced up through the dark behind me. It cut through the beam at an angle, spat against the black 'roof' a few feet above the temple, and winked out. The beam held, then slid past at the cut. The chimney fell. There were yells, and a scream came from below. The roof of the temple slid forward a foot - and stopped. Dust mushroomed up.

I was racing down the street to a cab parked a quarter of a block away. I couldn't help sparing a thought for the plight of the group in the reeling attic. I heard Cleopatra's curses as I was piled into a cab.

'The Tan Jet,' I told the driver. 'It's a kind of nightclub.'

'Yeah, I know,' the latter said in a voice heavy with knowledge, fixing on me the sad, resigned gaze one reserves for those who insist, against all excellent advice, on running towards their doom.

IX

Someone was singing 'Do You Know the Way to San José?' in a sultry, melancholy voice. I walked down a dark ramp and into the bright lights of the Tan Jet. No live or robot door attendant was on guard, at least no obvious one, and no hostess came hurrying up. Customers were expected to know their way around. There were a lot of them. They sat in small parties with a truculent quietness sneering at the frantic hustle of the times and the belief the hustle was leading the world nowhere. Four live musicians blew and strummed old jazz instruments while a single amber spotlight shone on the coffee coloured, languid songstress, whose sequined dress went all the way to her wrists and chin.

Do you know the way to San José?

I've been away so long

I may go wrong and lose my way

Do you know the way to San José?

I'm going back to find

Some peace of mind in San José

I spotted the dark sheen of Judy Womack's hair at the far end of the room. I walked toward her, a trifle uneasy.

In a week, maybe two

They'll make you a star

Weeks turn into years, how quick they pass

And all the stars that never were

Are parking cars and pumping gas

As the listeners hissed their applause, I stopped a few feet away from Judy's table. She was with three young men, with the quiet dignity of murderers. When Judy turned to see what they were looking at, she sprang up with the delighted cry of 'Maurice!' though there was alarm in her eyes. She walked over to me and slapped me with her left hand. I whipped up my hand to hit her back but hesitated and managed a sketchy pat. She turned around with a bright smile, saying, 'Maurice, meet Ralf, Florian, and Wolfgang.'

Ralf was so skinny his eyes were a single file. He wore a side parting, and I look that told you he was a German.

'So, this is the clown you blabbed tonight's plans to.'

Florian was also thin and German with a face like a haunted pencil. 'You seem to have told him we'd come here later,' he said. 'Puzzles me why he didn't bring the police.'

Wolfgang had a battered, scarred, flattened, thickened, checked, and welted face. It was a face that had nobody to fear. A look that'd had everything done to it that anybody could imagine.

'Police never tried to pick up anybody in the Tan Jet, yet', he observed. 'Not now, Cuts Like a Buffalo!' He addressed this last remark to a worn, mangy Alsatian that thrust its head from under his legs and snapped.

I snared an empty chair from the following table, found myself an empty glass, and filled it with the contents of a tall, slim pitcher. Like the others, Florian had a half-inch in the bottom of his drink, caught Wolfgang's attention, and rolled his eyes toward the ceiling. Ralf smoothed his parting like a judge might have adjusted his wig before giving a sentence.

'Judy, it's clear you spilt our plans to this clown, and he told the police, so they were waiting for us when we knocked over the first sales robot. And if I hadn't insisted on putting an extra charge in the rockets, they would have captured us.'

'It was a coincidence,'

'First time we ever had a coincidence. I don't believe there are such things.'

I took a deep drink. It seemed mild, sweet stuff, compared to the adulterated whiskey Cleopatra had fed me.

Dreams turn into dust and blow away

And there you are without a friend

You pack your car and ride away

 Ralf continued, 'Judy, we welcomed you into the Kummerspeck Gang, even though you were a psychoanalyst's daughter. You betrayed the gang tonight. Your irresponsibility lost us a wad of dough.' Ralf paused. 'You're out, Judy.'

Florian agreed.

'Yeah,' Wolfgang said, rubbing Cuts Like a Buffalo's snout.

I put my elbows on the table. 'Gentlemen,' I whispered, 'you say you are out a wad of dough? I can remedy that.'

Ralf looked at me with mild irritation.

'I am seeking a jewel beyond price,' I continued. 'To get it, I intend tonight to rob the premises of Love Incorporated. You can help me.'

At the mention of Love Incorporated, Wolfgang turned his head at least half an inch while Ralf blinked uncontrollably.

'You have big ideas, don't you?'

'Yeah,' Wolfgang agreed with a yawn. 'You could have picked an easier place.'

Ralf looked at Judy, 'You said he was one of your father's patients, didn't you?'

Judy went to reply, but I cut in,

'I know a private way into Love Incorporated, right through Mr Brimstone's office. So, it'll be simple.'

Wolfgang drawled, 'What is this jewel beyond price?'

'Something I wouldn't expect you to appreciate,' I took a less cautious slug of the mind swelling drink. 'There should be enough in the way of ordinary valuables lying about to compensate you for your effort. Love Incorporated is wealthy. All sales robots work from there. Why not hit them where they live?'

Cuts Like a Buffalo stretched from under Wolfgang's chair and snapped at my hand. Stiffened by the drink, I didn't move it. The jaws clashed an inch away. 'Why do you call it Cuts Like a Buffalo?'

Wolfgang explained with condescension. 'It's bred back to ancestors of the Cuts Like a Buffalo tribe.'

I wondered whether cats could be bred back to their Egyptian ancestors and whether those ancestors might have been blue.

In the pause, Judy's eyes grew bright. She looked at her companions. 'Why don't we take him up on it?' she said. 'I mean, robbing Love Incorporated sounds exciting.'

'It will be risky,' I cut in. 'Mr Treacle's boys have guns.'

'Why don't we go for it?' no one answered Judy's question. 'Well, I guess that's it,' she said with a triumphant smile, turning away from the table. 'Come on, Maurice, let's go!'

We had taken three steps when Ralf chuckled. I might have kept going, but Judy turned back with a repressed eagerness, and I resisted.

'Don't kill yourselves running,' Ralf said. 'Florian and Wolfgang and I are signing up for this little expedition, providing you can give us the right answers to a few questions when we get outside.' he smiled as he got up. 'One last thing, Judy. This time there better be no cops.'

Judy laughed. I accepted the situation with a 'Glad to have your help, boys,' and took Judy's arm, but she linked hers with those of Ralf and Florian, not sparing me another look.

The sequined singer shifted to a snappier rhythm.

Oh, L.A. is a great big freeway

Put a hundred down and buy a car

In a week, maybe two

They'll make you a star

Weeks turn into years, how quick they pass

And all the stars that never were

On the way out, I felt a sudden hand on my shoulder. I turned to see a black-haired, faun-like girl whose apartment window was opposite mine. I froze in every muscle, my hand locked to the ajar door, ready to jerk it open and run.

'Celeste?'

She greeted me with a smile. 'Hello,' she said in a warm foreign accent I couldn't place. 'Say, did you ever find that blue cat of yours?'

'No,' I said, 'but I'm going to.'

X

'And how did you plan to get inside when the place is closed for the night?' Ralf prodded sardonically.

I cocked my eyebrows defiantly and gave the restaurant door a smart shove. It swung silently inward. I led the way haughtily, vaguely aware that Florian was examining the lock.

The long room was gloomy. It smelled stalely of people and liquor and seared yams; I even thought I could distinguish Cleopatra's whiskey. Cuts Like a Buffalo snuffed eagerly and tugged Wolfgang forward by his leash. I steered their course confidently between the counter and the booths. I was feeling particularly pleased with myself.

'The lock was burned,' I heard Ralf whisper to Florian. 'Somebody's ahead of us. We must watch out.'

I pushed open the door to the stairs and hesitated. Inside it was now completely black. Something hissed softly beside me, and a luminescent cone puffed out. A couple of seconds later, the half dozen treads of the stairway glowed with a milky green sheen.

'Luminescent mist,' Florian explained with professional casualness. 'You get going. I'll spray.'

I started up the stairs, the milky surface light keeping two or three treads ahead of me in blobby advances. The mist got on Cuts Like a Buffalo so that he glowed like the Hound of the Baskervilles. Some of it even got on my trouser bottoms and moccasins.

'We're certainly marked if we have to run away and hide,' I muttered as I reached the corridor Cleopatra and I had come through and took the unknown way upward.

'Don't worry,' Wolfgang chuckled wisely, 'I'm spraying a neutralizer behind us.' He directed a dark, faintly hissing canister at my feet and my shoes blacked out, along with a blob of surrounding treads. Looking back, I saw the glow on the stairs vanish abruptly. I could not see Judy, Ralf, or Florian.

I asked Wolfgang, 'How do you manage two canisters and Cuts Like a Buffalo all at the same time?'

'Hell, I could aim a squirrel rifle and walk this beast at the same time,' Wolfgang assured me.

I became aware of a dim radiance above me, beyond the range of Wolfgang's mist. Wolfgang hurriedly neutralized all the luminescence, including that on Cuts Like a Buffalo. I cautiously went up the last ten treads, the upper radiance increasing all the while, and found myself in a shadowy, curving corridor. My steps got shorter and shorter, then stopped.

A couple of yards ahead lay three swollen furry shapes, each with a half dozen slim black things stuck into them, like feathered darts. I recognized at least two of the dead cats. Although grotesquely puffed up, their markings told me they were a Siamese and a shorthair I had seen at the temple.

'Watch it!' Ralf whispered, but at the same instant, Cuts Like a Buffalo jerked away from Wolfgang and lunged swiftly forward, his leash trailing to sniff at the nearest swollen shape. The tail of the dart next to Cuts Like a Buffalo's nose began to spin with a faint, feathery rustle. Cuts Like a Buffalo became tensely still, disregarding his master's anxiety, 'Back, Cuts Like a Buffalo!' The rustle became a buzz. Cuts Like a Buffalo suddenly snapped sideways at the dart, but the dart withdrew quickly from the dead cat at the same instant. Cuts Like a Buffalo's teeth clashed emptily. The dart hovered a few feet in the air like a vast black wasp. 'Don't anybody go closer,' Ralf ordered hoarsely. Wolfgang grabbed for the end of the leash. Still, it was snatched away from his hand when Cuts Like a Buffalo abruptly changed position, watching the dart with deadly intentness.

The hum became a loud sinister buzz. There were two quick *zings*, and the hovering dart trembled like a blown candle flame. Half turning, I saw that Ralf was shooting at it with some sort of air-gun. The dart began to waltz in little loops. Cuts Like a Buffalo leapt straight up and snapped at it as a dog might at a bee, but the dart curtsied away.

Wolfgang's 'Back, Cuts Like a Buffalo' was desperate. The dog stayed on its feet and batted at the dart with his paws. There were more futile *zings* from Ralf' airgun. Finally, the dart looped back and hovered in front of Cuts Like a Buffalo's muzzle. As he opened his jaws for a snap, it shot down his throat.

Cuts Like a Buffalo, his eyes and jaws open wide, beat the air with his paws. Then he dropped to all fours and hurled himself off at top speed. He slammed against a wall, got up with difficulty, trembled over to Wolfgang, and fell and didn't move. It seemed like the gaunt creature was taking a deep breath, and then suddenly, it began to swell.

'Don't touch him!' Ralf shouted, but Wolfgang was keeping his distance. Ralf came up beside Wolfgang and leaned prudently forward, his side parting swinging out from his forehead. 'Always did want to see one of those things in action,' he mumbled.

'They're what they call singular missiles, aren't they?' Florian asked fascinatedly. 'Anti-individual, I mean.'

Ralf nodded. 'Used them in the last cold war. They were for assassinations. They're supposed to be driven by a tiny, ion-emitting radioactive fan. I wish I had a counter so I could know. And of course, they home on the radiant heat of flesh and then inject a poison.'

Wolfgang muttered, 'Cuts Like a Buffalo.' The dog's swollen eyes turned toward him, then glazed over. Wolfgang jerked up and made a derisive noise. 'Always was a dumb pooch,' he said.

I started ahead, drugs battling nausea inside me so that the dim corridor seemed both vivid and unreal.

'Where are you going?' said Ralf.

'To find what I came for!'

'Well, keep away from the cats!'

'How do we know those singular missiles won't heat up and go for us as they went for Cuts Like a Buffalo?' he heard Wolfgang demand fretfully.

'The others got through, didn't they?' Ralf said irritably.

'What others?'

'The ones who burnt the lock on the door, the ones who threw the cats ahead of them to draw the missiles,' Ralf told him impatiently. 'Incidentally, if any of the missiles start spinning their tails, you might start by throwing your coat over them.'

Beyond the dead cats, we came to a silvery mesh barricade with several jagged cuts in it, three of them making a crude doorway. The mesh looked strong enough to have kept the wasps on this side. I stepped over the fallen section of mesh. The cut ends of the silvery wire were rounded and fused as if by great heat.

Just beyond the mesh lay a chunky man in a grey, company guard uniform. He had a gun in his hand. He was intact except that the top of his head had rolled about a foot away. It had been sliced off tidily just above the nose by something hot. I remembered how neatly the blue needle had sliced the steel beam. I hurried past toward an open arch just ahead and jerked back from a giant grey snake coiled there. Then I saw the snake was a robot doorman like Old Rubber arm, and looking higher. I saw someone had sliced it off close to the wall.

Judy and the rest came through the mesh. Ralf kneeled eagerly by the dead man and examined the gun he was clasping, but a moment later got up and grabbed me by the lapels of my jacket.

'Look here, clown,' he said. 'Who are those others? You must have known someone was going to break in here tonight. You were counting on that door being open.'

'Take it easy,' Florian said with a smiling flash of white teeth. 'Here's a bit of an odd thing. See where whatever sliced this robot arm cut into the wall beyond? Well, follow back from the cut in a straight line through the slice in the robot arm.'

Like the others, I followed Florian's directions and saw that the straight line ended in a deep cut in the floor a half dozen feet behind us.

'I don't get it,' Wolfgang said. 'You mean somebody shot some kind of beam from the next floor under us?'

'The evidence points to a gun that shoots in opposite directions at the same time. I fancy that if we'd have looked behind us at the head of the stairs, we'd have seen some cuts mirror-imaging those in the mesh.'

'Say, look at this here, communicator,' Wolfgang interrupted. He had been poking around the side of the corridor behind the guard. 'One button got a new-looking gadget rigged up to it that's pushed it twice now while I've been watching.'

'Don't touch it,' Ralf said. 'It's probably a button Headless here is supposed to thumb every so often to show he's on guard. Whoever broke in ahead of us knows their business. Once more, Maurice, who were they?'

'Yeah, talk,' Wolfgang said, coming up beside Ralf. 'I figure you're responsible for Cuts Like a Buffalo getting killed.'

'As do I,' Florian said, letting go of the stub arm which contracted toward the wall until it was like a wrinkled scar. While eerie and ominous tension held everyone else stock-still, I stumbled with drugged aplomb past Florian and through the arch.

'Gentlemen,' I said, 'I imagine you would like to inspect the treasure house.'

The room was so vast and lengthy that the only visible wall was the one against which we stood. It was not lit, yet it seemed so because of the brightness of the two sorts of ranked objects on which the light fell. To the left were a row of endless sales robots, shiny high turtle shapes with a smaller dome set on the main one, the same efficient metal hucksters daily and evening roaming the streets, guiding themselves and spotting customers by hypersonic radar and optical scanner. Only now, their fascinating windows for displaying samples were closed. Their money collecting commodity giving arms were folded, the restless wheels under their metal skirts were still, and their harmonious voices were rich with a restrained sex appeal suitable to robots.

To the right, there was a host of dress-display robots, arrayed in everything from high collared sable evening cloaks to bathing jewellery. Their hair gleamed with a hundred tints, their suede-rubber skins glowed with a creamy seductiveness, they held themselves with the poise of princesses, but as the sales robots, they were still. No slinky parading, no cute, individualized gestures, no mysterious or haughty smiles, no soft lips were opening to recite the qualities and prices of the garments they were modelling. They all stared straight ahead like Egyptian mummies not yet wrapped, and indeed, one, cased and clad in a filmy sheath, was a precise copy of Nefertiti.

It occurred to me the ranked sales robots and dress-display robots were a military display; I was looking at the armed might - the money army and the glamour army - of Love Incorporated.

Florian darted to the nearest sales robot and made some manipulations. Finally, there was a clinking, and he was waving a blue and silver handful and his teeth, and the whites of his eyes shone in his face.

'They're still carrying the day's cash!' I said.

Wolfgang looked from the money army to the glamour army with greedy indecision. When Ralf snorted, he trotted over to help Florian, who worked his way down the first row of sales robots.

Despite his greater self-control, it was clear Ralf's hands were itching too. 'Wake up, Judy,' he said. She turned toward him.

'Hey,' Wolfgang called in an exciting stage whisper. 'we're coming to the gambling robots.'

Ralf didn't go at once. He studied Judy. 'I want no more slip-ups.'

Though mute, her time seemed to satisfy him, and he rushed off to join Florian and Wolfgang.

I turned around and walked through an archway beside the one through which we had entered the room. I hadn't taken ten steps down the curving corridor before Judy whirled past me and positioned herself in my path.

'Get back,' she whispered - the hand directing a ten-inch knife at my chest.

'Judy,' I said. 'Your friends have found what they came for, but I haven't. Let me go.'

She advanced the knife, so it touched my shirt.

'You're going to let me go past,' I repeated, 'because you're not sure that being cruel and smart is the right way to face the world. You're not sure anymore. The approval of your gang is the only something that matters. It's a grudging approval, Judy, something you've had to sit up and do tricks like another dumb canine, and your comradeship with them isn't at all the romantic, until death, one for all and all that you pretend. But I don't have the time to tell you any more because I've got my own business, and I've got to get on with it.'

'Get back,' she snarled. But although the knife now pricked my chest, it was no longer a command but a plea.

'I'm going past now, Judy,' I walked ahead into the knife. It drew back at the same speed with which I walked into it for about two feet, whipped to one side as I passed Judy.

Neither of us made another sound. I looked back and saw her profile in the light from the enormous room and the slack line of her shoulder and the arm holding the knife. Often faces look weak, but I'd never seen one that looked so lost.

The curving corridor grew darker and lighter again, made a sharp turn, and emerged into a long, furnished room. I blundered a step forward before I saw three people at the far end, and one of them was Mr Treacle. They weren't looking for my way, and I could have ducked back out of sight enough. Still, I hurried it too much and brushed against a slim pillar topped by a small aquarium in which tiny pink, blue, and violet octopuses clung and swam. The pillar teetered. Stumbling, I grabbed to steady it, fell out into the room with it as the candy-coloured octopuses gushed out.

XI

After a couple of seconds, I decided keeping myself scrunched against the floor with both eyes closed would not help. So, I opened them, blinked at the flooring, and tried to nerve myself to look up.

'Mr Treacle, what's keeping that man from the FBI?' said a voice.

'Don't worry. He'll be here any minute.'

'What if they're lying and planning to raid us?

'The government wouldn't dare do that. They need the blue cat, or they think they do.'

'Then why isn't the FBI man here?'

'Try not to worry. Relax. Let Pandora stroke your forehead.'

I lifted my chin off the floor and swivelled my head. The Mr Brimstone I'd heard mentioned with so much awe turned out to be a gaunt, dark man who looked at first glance thirty, at second seventy, and at third a mystery to which youth-prolonging hormones might give a clue. He dressed in a pinstripe waistcoat that swelled like the sail of a racing yacht. Mr Treacle was much larger physically, but his stature had shrunk to a servant with privileges. Even his black glasses looked comical.

The other person in the room was a beautiful violet blonde whose dress comprised an endless spiral of fine silver wire over a white satin sheath. She was sitting at a table, watching the others with a stiff smile.

But the one overwhelming fact was none of them was paying any attention to me. My crashing into the room with the aquarium hadn't been of enough importance to raise a glance. Besides being mystified and frightened, I was slightly annoyed.

'You shouldn't take that attitude toward Pandora,' Mr Treacle said. 'She's a brilliant girl, so clever! Isn't that right, Pandora?'

'I am skilled in giving pleasure to men and women,' said Pandora. 'I have memorized all the important erotic fiction written since the dawn of history.'

'Treacle, you still don't appreciate how serious this is. According to my latest information, the government is all set to indict not only three of our governors and a hundred of our mayors but four of our national senators and a dozen of our representatives.'

'That would mean the absolute finish of Love Incorporated.'

'And what have I been saying to you?'

I settled my chin on the back of my right hand to watch them. This manoeuvre attracted no attention. I gave up trying to figure it out.

Mr Treacle recovered his spirits.

'Anyway, you've got the blue cat, so you're safe.'

'Have I got it?' Mr Brimstone demanded. 'Where is that cat locked up, Treacle?'

'It's in a copper cage where nobody can get at it, and it can't get at anybody. Besides, it's still stunned.'

Mr Brimstone was pacing. 'But why should the FBI want it? It's a funny coloured animal. It makes little sense.'

'We've been through this before, Mr Brimstone. They're convinced the cat is dangerous. It can control minds and change personalities, including the four top officials who've skipped the country and headed for China. The government believes the cat is a mutant or monster and can conquer the country - the entire world even - by controlling thoughts and feelings.'

'The cat showed nothing peculiar to me. It's all a grade-A delusion, a top-secret panic. Now, where is that FBI man?'

'On his way. Everything's going to turn out all right.'

'That's what you said when the president first took action against Love incorporated,' Mr Brimstone flared. 'You said it was a bluff. You told me McCarthy was a drunken farmer who could be got at twenty ways. You told me it would all blow over.'

'I know,' said Treacle for once at a loss for easy words.

'Do you know what happened?' Mr Brimstone pressed.

 'McCarthy is nuts!'

'That's your explanation for everything! If something happens this time, do you suppose I'll be happy because you tell me the officers arresting me are nuts? Where *is* the FBI man?'

'You should try to relax. Distract yourself with Pandora here.'

Treacle looked at Pandora's waxen beauty.

'Fix your lipstick,' he said.

The violet, blonde beauty slid from the table and came straight toward me.

'Check out that slinky walk.' Mr Treacle urged. 'What a gorgeous babe, eh?'

She tossed her head, stopped six feet short of me, took out a lipstick, looked straight ahead of her, and made up her lips. Something cold and sucking closed on the fingers of my left hand. I flipped it, and a tiny pink octopus sailed through the air toward the girl and flattened itself against something in the air about two feet short of her.

I watched it clinging there, and my mind swelled to bursting as if I'd had another shot of Tan Jet lemonade. I got up, walked forward, and found an invisible flat surface extending between me and the other half of the room. I was on the viewing side of a one-way mirror bisecting the room. Pandora was standing so close I could have touched her. She turned and her skirt brushed the other side of the surface. It was at least two inches from the side to which the octopus still clung. I realised I must not be hearing their voices with a new surprise, but a miked and transmitted version of them.

I looked back along the corridor I'd travelled and ahead along its darker and straighter continuation on my side of the panelled-out room. Why should Mr Brimstone have the sound turned on so I could spy on him? It made no sense.

I might have left the spy chamber, but Mr Treacle put down a phone and said, 'He's coming!'

Mr Brimstone at once stopped pacing and became calm. He did not look at the archway beyond him, though Treacle did. A man came through the archway and stopped.

Mr Brimstone looked at him with a questioning smile, just short of a smirk. He waited, then whispered. 'Under the circumstances, I suppose you do not care to use your name?'

'My name is Special Agent Stone,' the other said.

'Have they empowered you to deal on behalf of the president?'

The other nodded once.

'Agent Stone, Mr Treacle,' Mr Brimstone said with a gracious wave of his arm, like the swaying of a snake. 'Agent Stone, Pandora.'

The government man acknowledged the introductions.

'Mr Brimstone,' he said. 'You tell us you have the blue cat. If you have, the government will buy it from you.'

'And what will you pay?'

'The Moreland-McCartney letters, proving the grant those senators received from Love Incorporated, plus all related recording and microwave taps. Also, similar material in sixty-odd other cases.'

'Not enough,' said Mr Brimstone.

'Of course, I could appeal to you finer nature,' Agent Stone said. 'The country and the citizens of this entire hemisphere are facing a deadly danger!'

'Please, Agent Stone.'

'Letters of confidence on all the indicted officials, dated today and signed and thumb printed by the president and all the service heads, confirming vocal recordings and pictures of the recordings being made. Our experts will have to examine the cat before they made the exchange. They can be here in twenty minutes.'

'That's better. But not enough.'

'What else do you want?'

'The witnesses, delivered into our hands,' said Mr Brimstone. 'And the thirty-odd - no, I'll be precise - thirty-four others.'

'That's out,' said Agent. 'I can't pay you in human lives.'

'Who mentioned anything like that?' It's just we'd feel safer with the witnesses in our protective custody rather than yours.'

'I know what you'd do to them,'

'You wouldn't have to think about it. There are ways to forget.' He glanced at Pandora, who flashed the FBI man a lazy, provocative smile.

Agent Stone flushed. For a few seconds, he seemed to concentrate on the wedding ring on his left hand.

'Look here,' he said. 'Don't get the idea either the government or I have anything but loathing for you. Love Incorporated has corrupted a third of a nation. We have your headquarters here and in twenty cities so well cordoned a wasp couldn't get out. The sole reason we haven't smashed you is you tell us you've captured something a little more dangerous to the country than even your rotten organization. But our patience is wearing thin. We suspect a bluff, despite those blue hairs you sent us. Make a deal while you can.'

'The chemical and physical analysis of the hair must have shown your experts something exciting. Like you say, Special Agent Stone, we have something you can't do without. Something worth - shall we say, a third of a nation? We are letting you off. Consider what the Chinese might pay. So, I'm afraid the witnesses are an essential part of the exchange.'

'I'm warning you,' Stone flared, 'I'm in full charge of Project Blue Kitty under J. Robert Oppenheimer, and I've advised both him and the president to break off the deal and raid if you insist on other conditions.'

'I'm only interested in what McCarthy and Oppenheimer have advised.'

Stone looked as if he wished he were deaf and dumb. His hands clenched and unclenched. Finally, he set himself to speak as a phone light blinked. Mr Treacle snatched it up, prepared to roar out a rebuke and slam it down. Instead, he listened and kept on listening. Stone watched him.

I heard the soft kiss of a door slitting open and faint footsteps drabber in quality than the binaural richness of the stuff I'd been listening to. I looked down the straight dark corridor on my side of the panel - forty feet down, where it ended in light. I saw Dr Womack cross the corridor carrying a black bag. In his other hand was a gun.

Mr Brimstone grabbed the phone from Mr Treacle with a glare.

'Three of them?' Mr Brimstone's words were staccato. 'And a fourth man and a girl, they said? And what did they tell you the fourth man wanted? I don't care if it sounds silly! *What?*'

Holding the phone, Mr Brimstone spared Agent Stone a glance. 'We're going to have to delay making final arrangements for a few minutes,' he said. 'Pandora will entertain you.'

'You can't delay,' Stone assured him with a note of triumph. 'The raid is in ten minutes unless I return. Besides, there's only one something important enough to make you interrupt this interview. You've lost the blue cat.'

'Oppenheimer would allow more time.'

'Let me contact Mr Oppenheimer,' Stone said. 'We'll cooperate with you in finding the cat. You have my word it will quash the indictments.'

'That's a good one.'

Mr Brimstone lifted the phone. But before he'd got it to his ear and mouth, the skin around his eyes contracted with suspicion. He gazed toward me or instead toward a point near me.

The two first fingers of Mr Brimstone right hand struck like a serpent's fangs at two buttons. Lights flared around me, everything was still, and I caught myself in a bright mirror that hid Mr

Brimstone and halved the length of the room. My reflection had the expression of a man caught naked in public. I hesitated for another desperate second, then ran down the straight corridor. In the end, I whisked around the corner in the direction Dr Womack had gone until I heard footsteps ahead and pounding toward me. I darted back the way Dr Womack had come and found myself in a room occupied by a heavy copper cage with less than an inch between the bars.

I looked around for a way out.

The circling look ended at the door through which I'd come. Mr Brimstone and Mr Treacle were standing in it. Treacle held a gun, Mr Brimstone, a laser.

'All right,' he said. 'What have you done with the blue cat?'

XII

It couldn't have been three minutes since my capture, but it felt like I had been listening to Mr Brimstone for years. I sat on a stool in a long low room with two men in blue tracksuits whom Mr Brimstone addressed as George and Elroy. Along one of the long sides of the room were windows and a doorway leading onto a balcony beyond which yawned impenetrable darkness. George and Elroy stood behind me while Mr Brimstone paced in front, his curving waistcoat preceding him like the advance guard of a royal procession.

'Have you ever imagined having $10,000,000? A yacht on the Amazon? Bubble-dome cabin? A private copter, a blonde, a brunette, or a red-headed robot. Doesn't it appeal to you?'

'I didn't take the blue cat,' I said. 'I don't know where it is.'

'What do you want for a ransom? Tell me. I've heard everything.'

I said nothing.

'Hit him, George,' Mr Brimstone ordered. 'And don't be all day about it!'

Pain bounced like a steel ball back and forth inside my skull at George's blows. At the last one, I felt my head go numb and my eyes glassy.

Mr Brimstone produced the laser he'd been carrying.

'I propose to cut your limbs off, one by one. The beam burns, which keeps you from bleeding too fast.'

All my glazed mind could consider was how ludicrous the word 'limb' was. Did Mr Brimstone think of me as a tree? Mr Brimstone circled like a minor planet, though it may only have been the room spinning. I stuck out an arm.

'All right,' I said, 'But don't hurt the leaves.'

Mr Brimstone lowered the gun. 'You hit him too hard, George. Where's Mr Treacle? I told him he had two minutes to find Hercules. Elroy, frisk this man.'

Slim fingers rippled through my pockets. I had a late memory when the hand went for my right-hand pocket and moved to prevent it, but George grabbed me. Elroy handed Mr Brimstone the figurine of Judy Womack.

Mr Brimstone rattled it to Elroy.

'I'd swear that nun made this - the one who used to do striptease dolls for us. She always had a touch. It's got better,' he ran his fingers over the doll. 'Would it pain you to see her hurt?' He set it on a table beside him and threw up his hands. 'Where *is* Treacle!'

'Here,' the latter announced, hulking into the room like a bear in a great hurry. 'I've located Hercules. And we've caught the girl the three Germans blabbed about. She lined herself up with the dress-display robots and might have passed herself off as one before she sneezed.'

They marched Judy into the room, her hands twisted behind her by Pandora, whose face wore a disdainful smile. The analyst's daughter had lost her evening cape, and her long dark hair hung half over one eye. She held her chin up, like someone who has struggled, found it no use, but not submitted. She saw me and looked away as if her being caught had wiped out the problem I had put her in.

'Ah, the original,' Mr Brimstone observed, looking up from the figurine, which I pocketed.

'Darling,' he said. 'Would you care to be featured in coast-to-coast living adverts or sit for a line of ultra-deluxe dress-display robots? Would you like to be a star, ambassadress to Brazil, or become my girl Friday and be in on everything interesting in the world? Or would you take the $10,000,000? Now, tell us what you've done with the blue cat.'

Judy answered with a shrug of her upper lip.

'Darling, I'm serious. This is a lifetime opportunity, and you're a delightful girl.'

He made out to caress her shoulder but whipped around to catch my reaction.

Hercules Jones ran into the room and whisked to a stop. He glanced at me as if he didn't know me and saluted Mr Brimstone.

'What are you standing around for?' said Mr Brimstone. 'Get to work. I want those three Germans in here.'

I tried to squirm away from George's casual grip. But felt Hercules's fingers were digging at my nerves, and the pain was like a fiery plant's red-hot roots and million rootlets finding an instant way through every crevice between the cells of my body.

'Dr Womack! Womack!' I babbled. 'Dr Womack stole the cat. I saw him coming out of the room where the cage is, carrying a black bag. The cat must have been inside.'

'Who is Dr Womack?' said Mr Brimstone.

'An analyst.' I nodded at Hercules Jones. 'He can tell you about him.'

'I've never heard of the man,' said Hercules.

'You did,' I said. 'You saw he was after me tonight. He must have guessed I was after the blue cat.'

Hercules shook his head. 'He's making it up. He's a nut.'

I looked at Judy.

'Dr Womack is my father,' she said. 'Reputed to be a great psycho-analyst. This nut you're wasting time on is one of his patients.'

'Darling, why didn't you say so before?' said Mr Brimstone. 'Pandora, let go of her wrists at once!' The violet blonde complied with a cynical hop of her slim eyebrows.

'Darling, it escaped my mind; she was still doing that. I'm sorry,' Mr Brimstone glided towards Judy, his feet moving as glibly as his tongue. 'Darling, it's obvious to me now: this lunatic stole the cat and handed it to your father. Now tell us where he is, and you'll have all of those things I mentioned to you a half-minute ago.'

'My father hasn't skill enough to burgle a banana,' Judy snapped at him. 'You're as stupid and arrogant and unbalanced as him. Just because something clever happened, a man must have done it. My father's a rotten analyst, but you could use a few sessions with him.'

Judy's right hand was a blurred arc, and Mr Brimstone sashayed back with four bright red lines on his left cheek.

'Grab her, Pandora!' he said. The violet blonde wrapped her arms around Judy's waist and elbows. Meanwhile, Mr Brimstone was rapid firing, 'Get those claws off her.' Treacle grabbed Judy's right hand around the knuckles with one of his giant paws and jerked off the needle-fanged thimbles.

Mr Brimstone paced back toward Judy. 'Darling,' he said, and for once, the words came slowly. 'You're the sort of charming vixen a sadist dreamed up to torture the hero. But tonight, I'm afraid you're going to have to reverse roles.'

My inner tormentor, who had made me go up against Mr Treacle at the temple, now got to work again. Despite the weakness of my pain-threaded muscles, it forced me into a staggering rush at Mr Brimstone; while calling out, 'Don't you touch her!'

Hercules tripped me and caught me by the collar before I'd smashed into the floor. He scooped me up and slammed me back onto the stool. Even I thought that was impressive.

Elroy and four or five other men marched a banged-up Ralf, Florian, and Wolfgang into the room's far end. Ralf, who now had blood trailing down his forehead, stared at Judy.

'Thank you for this,' he said.

Florian and Wolfgang each nodded their head.

'You take it for granted I ratted on you?' said Judy. None of the three Germans acted as if they'd heard the question.

'Take those boys down to the company garage,' Mr Brimstone called to Elroy. 'I'll phone you orders about them in fifteen seconds.' Elroy and the guards jumped to obey, 'Thanks again, darling,' Mr Brimstone said to Judy in a loud voice for Ralf to hear. He had time to give her one last deadly look before the guards hurried him out with the others.

'Come on, everybody,' said Mr Brimstone. 'We're going to have some entertainment. Darling, would you like to take my arm? If you promise to be a good girl, I'll tell Pandora to let go of you.'

Judy made no reply, but Pandora unwrapped her arms with lazy reluctance.

'Come on, darling,' Mr Brimstone entreated, heading for the balcony. Judy didn't look at him, but she walked to his side. He didn't touch her. They moved fast. Mr Brimstone looked back over his shoulder.

'Hurry, everybody!'

Mr Treacle, Pandora, and George fell in behind them. Hercules brought up the rear with me.

'I had to do that,' Hercules whispered in my ear. 'I couldn't fake it and trust you to fake reactions well enough to fool Mr Brimstone. For God's sake, say nothing more about Dr Womack. Womack made me bring him here. My friends are at the house. They'll kill the nun and the monk - Cleopatra and Virgil, too - If he gets caught.'

As I tried to answer this, we followed the others onto the balcony. Its railing split by a gateway, from which a metal stairway projected down and out into the darkness, its first dozen treads glimmering.

Without warning, Judy darted down the stairs, taking them three at a time. George lunged after her, but Mr Brimstone stopped him with a gesture. 'She's doing what I want and five times faster than if you dragged her. It's the speed I need.'

Mr Treacle was watching Judy, who was now only a glimmering moth flitting through duller darkness. 'She can't see the steps anymore,' he said with professional admiration. 'She's excellent at what she does.'

Mr Brimstone stepped to a control panel in the railing. He picked up a phone and paused as if he were making sure it was a full fifteen seconds since he spoke to Elroy and not a mere twelve or thirteen.

'Elroy?' Mr Brimstone paused, writhing his eyebrows, though Elroy was slow in catching on. 'Of course, of course!'

He touched a button, and a blinding light transformed the darkness into a vast, empty, grey garage, its floor thirty feet below the balcony. Many lines and signs showed how cars should move and park, only there weren't any cars. There were a dozen open gateways in the grey walls, eight of them marked 'Exit.' The silvery stairs down which Judy had flown touched the centre point of the garage's vast floor? A few paces away, Judy stood tiny and stock-still as if blinded by the light.

Somewhere, far off, an electric motor was revving up.

'Ladies and gentlemen,' said Mr Brimstone. 'This is the place where people park their cars while they watch the wrestling bouts. But now the wrestling's over, and the cars are all gone.' He touched his cheek, where the four furrows had stopped bleeding. 'So now we can have the place for our little piece of entertainment. Mr Tillet, you must have the blue cat. I believe you value that girl's beauty and life.'

Down below, Judy seemed to come out of her daze. She darted towards the nearest open gateway. I looked at Mr Brimstone and his dark fingers lifting. I looked back at Judy and saw her hesitate and run around toward the silvery stairs. Mr Brimstone touched another button, and the stairs retracted, telescoping upward. Judy stood on the grey floor all alone.

The revving of the unseen motor grew louder. Mr Brimstone leaned over the guard wall and regarded Judy as if he were a cleverer Caligula or a more practical Nero. He turned back and took the figurine of Judy out of my pocket.

'Mr Tillet,' he said, 'I want to know where the blue cat is or where your Dr Womack has taken it. Otherwise, would you like this to happen to her down there?' He jerked off a leg of the figurine. 'Or this?' Mr Brimstone jerked off an arm. 'Or this, or this?'

An open-topped black jeep came speeding up out from under the balcony. There were three people in it, though I couldn't tell who. But Judy darted toward the car, calling out, 'Ralf!' The vehicle came forward faster and straight toward her, and she had to dive out of the way to keep from being hit.

The car swung around in a great loop. Judy picked herself up from the floor.

'Or *this!*' Mr Brimstone hissed as he ripped the figurine apart at the waist, 'Now, tell me where Dr Womack is.'

'I don't know!' I yelled, struggling to get away from Hercules, who whispered in my ear.

'Don't say a word.'

'I'll remind you,' Mr Brimstone continued, taking something else from under his coat. 'It's much worse for her to be hurt by people she likes than by people she hates. So, tell me about the blue cat. Look here. This is a laser. I can cut down that car at any moment.'

But I, like all the others, was watching Judy. Having picked herself up, she didn't move. She stayed there, facing the oncoming car. It veered and missed her by an inch. Judy stood motionless, a statue. She turned at the waist and watched the retreating jeep.

'Chicken!' she jeered.

Mr Treacle was pounding the railing and saying, 'I tell you, that girl's good.'

Mr Brimstone turned to me. 'They're bound to get her unless....' He wiggled the large black gun he held in his tiny hand. 'So, you better talk.'

The jeep swung around under the balcony in a much tighter loop and headed back, revving. Judy faced it, grinning, hands light on her hips before. From my point of view, it had swallowed her up to the waist. She sprang to one side. Her foot must have brushed the tire. The jeep slammed through the air where she'd been.

'*Coward!*' Judy screamed.

Mr Brimstone, George and Pandora leaned forward over the guard rail.

'Look, Mr Tillet,' Mr Brimstone said, 'I don't want to see this girl smashed, but this is the last chance you have to save her. Where's Dr Womack? Where's the blue cat?'

I didn't even look at him.

A phone light blinked on the control panel. Mr Brimstone ignored it. '*Where's the blue cat?*'

The black jeep turned by the far wall. Judy pivoted to face it - all I could think of was that this had happened before, in ancient Crete, where girls like Judy had met the black, charging bull and vaulted over its cruel horns.

The phone light continued to blink.

The jeep finished its tight turn, Florian and Wolfgang leaning out to balance it like a sailboat while Ralf stuck steady death behind the wheel. It shrieked toward Judy. She waited until it was as close as the time before, then sprang toward the left. The jeep veered toward the left, too. Judy's feet, slamming down after the first jump, didn't carry her farther but reversed her direction, holding her back to the spot she'd first occupied.

Again, the jeep slammed past her.

'*Idiots!*' Judy said.

The jeep, screaming into another tight turn, vanished under the balcony. There was a grating crash and a sick, rasping sound as if the jeep had sideswiped the wall but was still going.

A dark shouldered pink topped figure walked out from under the balcony. It was carrying a black bag. It stopped, leaned over, set the black bag on the floor, and opened it.

The black jeep came out from under the balcony, gaining speed.

Something blue and small stuck its head out of the black bag and looked toward the jeep.

The jeep didn't stop, but it slowed, and Ralf, Florian and Wolfgang tumbled out and sprinted away from the blue head as if from horror.

The jeep continued toward Judy like a blinded, injured animal.

The pink topped figure walked back under the balcony as if it didn't know what it was doing. I realised it must be Dr Womack.

The phone light went on blinking.

The blue cat leapt out of the black bag and settled itself beside it.

'Stun it!' said Mr Brimstone.

The blue cat twisted its neck and looked up.

Mr Treacle and George looked at Mr Brimstone, and each took a step and peered down over the railing and stopped. Behind them, Pandora was pale and quiet, a ghost.

I felt it too - the same invisible golden wave of amiability and good feeling that had quieted the quarrellers at the temple but now in flood.

'Stun that stupid cat!' Mr Brimstone demanded. The hidden wrinkles were showing themselves twitchingly on his face, and he was backing away from the railing if he couldn't bear the golden wave.

Treacle picked up the phone beside the blinking light. After a moment, he said, 'The raid's started, just as Special Agent Stone told us it would. The FBI is coming in everywhere!'

'Stun it, I tell you!' Mr Brimstone ordered, fanning the air in front of my face as if to beat off the golden wave.

George looked at him. Mr Treacle shook his head. Mr Brimstone gave a shuddering gasp, clapped his free hand over his mouth and nostrils and fought his way to the railing. With his other hand, he raised the big gun until it was high above his shoulder.

A needle of blue light jutted from either end of the big gun and made smoking trenches in the opposite wall of the garage and the wall behind them. Mr Brimstone brought the weapon forward, lengthening the forward and rearward channels. The air turned acidic as if laced with ozone. The blue beam dimmed the bright lights and made everything shadowy.

The blue cat looked up at Mr Brimstone. But Mr Brimstone didn't look straight back at it. Instead, the tiny muscles in his jaw bulged, clamping shut his mouth and nose.

The forward trench dug across the wall and floor, swung past Judy and the doddering jeep, got ten feet from the blue cat and hesitated. It turned this way and that, as if it had encountered a magic circle it couldn't pierce - then stopped.

Mr Brimstone gave a great gasp and squealed.

The blue beams winked out. The gun rattled on the floor. Mr Brimstone swayed, and Hercules jumped to catch him.

I sprang forward and hit the buttons I'd seen Mr Brimstone touch. The bars in the garage gateways shot up. I was on the telescoped stairs. I rode them to the ground through layers of stinging ozone and golden harmony. The jeep had trembled to a stop short of Judy, who stared at it, her whole figure slack as if a puff of wind could have knocked her over.

When the stairs touched the floor, momentum carried me forward a half-dozen steps, but I kept my footing and circled back at a run when I plunged into the area between the blue cat and the spot where they abandoned the jeep.

In the next instant, I was calling, 'Zen!' and Zen was saying 'Prrt!' and I was scooping up the unresisting cat, my fingers trembling as they touched the blue fur and darting back toward Judy and the jeep. Her groggy look had now become a dazed smile of triumph and pride.

I grabbed her by the elbow and pulled her toward the jeep.

'Get in!' I shouted. 'We're getting out of here. You're driving.'

Life came back into her hands as she touched the wheel. I scrambled in beside her with Zen clutched to my chest.

'Which way?'

With a wheezy hum, the jeep sped toward the nearest gateway. I felt a thinning of the golden peace around us as if Zen were resting. The group on the balcony was still standing as motionless as display dummies with the power off - all except Mr Brimstone, who was once again moving about.

'Get them,' he said as he darted from one to the other. 'Kill them.'

The jeep nosed through the high doorway and up a ramp.

'Pandora!' yelled Mr Brimstone. 'Kill them.'

The next second, a blue beam flashed, and smoke and starry splatter sprayed up behind the jeep. The beam moved up and met the top of the gateway. It notched, came a little closer but stopped by the thickness of the wall. The ramp turned, and I saw a half-dozen men in the Love Incorporated company guard uniform. Two of them had drawn their guns and seemed to argue about something. They turned and saw the jeep. The two with guns raised them, and the others reached for theirs.

Zen sat upon my lap straight as the statuette of Bastet, and I felt him let go of another of those tremendous golden invisible waves. I could tell the moment it hit the guards from the change in their stern expressions. They watched the jeep with awe and incredulous grins.

Further on, we approached an expanse of grey cold light, against which a party of twenty-armed men were silhouetted. They levelled their weapons, but once again and mightier than ever, so potent it made me shiver, the golden wave rolled forward to engulf them. Once again, as the jeep glided, astonished and troubled faces smiled despite themselves. The jeep rolled out into the cool, shadowy dawn. I stroked Zen's soft, springy fur and murmured, 'Little peacemaker. You even calmed the FBI.'

Zen looked up at me, yawned and curled up on my lap. The golden harmony subsided until only a ghost of it lingered.

'I know,' I said. 'you're tired from all this peace-making. I'm tired myself. But I don't care whether you come from Egypt, China, or the jungles of the Amazon -you're good for me.'

XIII

The jeep turned corners, putting block after block of empty, early morning streets between us and Love Incorporated. Zen was a plump blue doughnut on my lap, radiating a kind of warm sleepy feeling. Before drifting off, I glanced at Judy. Her face was stern in proud, sneering lines, though two tears were jiggling down her cheeks.

'I admired your bravery dodging the jeep,' I said. 'It showed what sort of glorious criminal fellowship you had with those three Germans. I suspect you've discovered your romantic worship of evil isn't worth a finger snap in the face of genuine love and understanding.'

Judy let the car jog to a stop in a bumpy, blind end driveway in a neglected, shrubby square with tall buildings set around. I leaned back, smiling, my fingers playing with Zen's fur. I was waiting for Judy's sobs.

Instead, the door of the jeep slammed.

I looked around. Judy was standing outside the jeep against a shadowy background of misty, silent skyscrapers.

She leaned forward toward me, bracing herself against the door with stiff arms. Now, I told myself, it must happen. She must yield to Zen's power.

'I hate you, Maurice. You just want to see me turn to jelly.' New tears spurted from the inside corners of her eyes, but her expression grew fiercer. 'Ralf, Florian and Wolfgang may have tried to kill me, but at least they gave me a chance to be something. They gave me the dignity of being hated. They didn't drown me in slop.'

She went on in a voice that should have sounded choked, except she wouldn't let it. 'I want my kind of glory, no matter how cheap and selfish you think that is because it's the only thing shining and brave in a shoddy, cowardly world.'

I wondered why Zen's power was so slow in taking effect on her.

I ran my hand over Zen's fur.

'Wake up.'

Zen purred. Or it was a slight snore.

'Goodbye, Maurice,' said Judy.

'No, wait!' I hunched forward in my seat. 'Don't go yet.' I shook the blue cat again. 'Wake up, Zen,' I demanded. 'Stop her.'

The minor god hung in my hands like a limp blue rag.

I put Zen down on the seat beside me and got out of the car. But a wave of deep melancholy washed over me. Something precious was slipping away, but I didn't know whether I had the right to stop it. My god had failed me.

So, I watched Judy slipping away and did nothing except lift Zen back on my lap. She walked off along the misty shrubs, proud and angry, holding her back straight and her head high.

For what seemed a long time, I watched the dim, empty corner around which she had turned. Then, finally, it occurred to me that Zen might not have helped Judy because my earlier exertions had drained his powers; minor gods couldn't exude several great golden waves without suffering slight after-effects.

It occurred to me that I must be the subject of frantic searches by the Federal Bureau of Investigation, Love Incorporated's thugs, Dr Womack, and friends, and even good old Ralf, Florian and Wolfgang. Yet, I felt no fear nor any inclination to form a plan.

Four feet defined themselves in the doughnut-shaped pressure on my lap. Zen stretched, shook himself, looked up at me with the brightest eyes, and said, 'Prrrt-prt.'

'You're a fine sort of cat,' I said. 'Going to sleep when I needed you most.'

Zen disregarded these criticisms. 'Prrrrt-prt,' he repeated.

But now, my hypnotic daze was broken. I was once again sleepy. 'I know,' I mumbled at the blue blur beyond the shimmering fence of my eyelashes. 'You're hungry. Well, I suppose you deserve a feed after all you did. But I have got no cranberry sauce right now. I'll get you some something to eat … later … on.'

'Prrrt-prt!' Zen demanded in the outraged tones of an employee who finds himself cheated of his wages.

But I was beyond any appeal. 'Goodnight,' I said in the kindliest possible way and dropped off to sleep.

I dreamed of something far off and strange and ominous. I dreamed of dark forests and small animals screeching. The screeches grew louder, and I fled out of my dream altogether into the jeep parked in the blind end driveway in the little square.

I saw the ghosts of dark trees and heard the echo of the dream screeches for a moment. I realised the former was the square's unpruned shrubs, while the latter were the squeals and cries of schoolgirls scattering out of a building.

They must have come from school—no, from afternoon school, since the sunlight wasn't slanting at all into the square, and I must have slept there undisturbed all day.

I became aware my lap and heart were cold, and Zen was gone.

XIV

My first impulse was to jump out of the jeep and hunt around. But the chill in my heart told me Zen was further away. Besides, the place was a jungle, and one man could hunt through it forever for anything cat-size. I did not recognize the square, but I guessed I was in an intellectual residential neighbourhood judging by the schoolgirls. At first, the school was for girls, but I noticed a few lone boys among the homeward-bound students. There was an appearance of shabbiness in the streets. The skyscrapers were low, billboards lifeless and there were no cars.

My gaze roamed over the tiers of tiny flats, wondering where Zen might have gone. As I did so, I turned on the jeep's radio.

'... Mr Brimstone, mastermind of Love Incorporated, has fled the country. Tonight at 8:30, President McCarthy will speak to the nation to silence the small, syndicate-inspired clamour at the outlawing of male-female wrestling. As well as the full reasons behind the charges brought this morning by the federal government against sixty-nine top officials. Experts predict the president will reveal that Love Incorporated has been peddling dream drugs, temporary sterility tabs and female robots equipped for improper functioning.

Now, here's a news flash on the cat story. The cats are not carrying infection and are under no circumstances to be destroyed, whether owned, stray, or alley cats. There's a stiff jail sentence waiting for anyone who kills a cat. All owned cats must be brought to the nearest security station. Any person sighting a stray or alley cat must do the same.'

I cleared my mind, trying to put myself in Zen's place, for the direction he may have wandered off in. Instead, my head spun like a compass needle. I climbed out of the jeep and walked straight ahead, not turning away for the dusty, crackling shrubs but pushing through them.

I parted a final hedge and looked across the empty street at a house not as old as the temple but with a free sky above it. Built of ancient brick, it was three stories tall and looked respectable. It reposed onto a weedy terrace over the square surrounded by a high iron fence and was otherwise unremarkable except for the saucer-shaped object fifty feet across the roof. It looked like the house was wearing a blue beret and daring anyone to notice it.

I crossed the street, mounted steps, and peered through the iron gate. Besides the house's old-fashioned knob door, I made out a tarnished bronze plate that read:

Institute for Advanced Study.

I looked back. Where I figured the jeep to be, I could see the heads and black-clad shoulders of two men. The black reminded me of the clothes worn by Mr Brimstone and his yes men. One of them took a step up as if they were getting into the jeep, but the other pulled him back, and they hurried off - but not in my direction, I noted with relief.

I gave the iron gate a little push. It opened with a rusty 'Harrumph' that made me shrink. But nothing else happened, so after a minute, I slipped through and peered around at the undergrowth and to wander through it, calling softly for 'Zen!'

I looked back in the jeep's direction, and once I saw the TV-helmeted heads and blue shoulders of three police officers. I wondered if the next time I looked, I'd see Dr Womack, or the monk and the nun, or Ralf, Florian, and Wolfgang, and I shivered thinking how close I'd come to being caught by one of them.

But the next shock I got came from something nearer. I had rounded the house, after having poked through its lifeless and overgrown back yard, when I saw a man peering at me through the fence.

The most disturbing thing about the man was how much he resembled Celeste. The girl with hoofs. This man had the same vital, faun-like expression.

I froze. But the man yawned, turned away, and shuffled off, humming or hooting a little melody that gave me goose pimples because it reminded me of something from a dream.

The total experience was becoming dreamlike: the silent house, the neglected garden, the futile searching, the melancholy memory of Judy's leaving, the powerful sense of a dead past. But the feeling Zen was near was still so strong.

I mounted the steps to the front, reached for the knob, and put off the evil moment a little longer, calling 'Zen!' a few times along the shallow porch to either side.

'Are you looking for a cat?'

I spun around and faced an older man, tall and frail, a ghost, and a silent one since I hadn't heard him coming up the path. Nevertheless, his thick, wrinkle-netted face was familiar. I liked him at first sight.

The old man said, 'My interest is academic or childish curiosity, which comes to the same thing. Is it by any chance a blue cat? 'No, you don't have to answer the question, at least not any more than you have.' he beamed at me. 'You're a journalist, or at least we can pretend you are. Country Joe always calls in the press when we make a discovery, though I'm sorry to say the press stopped coming about twenty years ago. They'd stopped thinking of extrasensory perception as newsworthy. But there's been time to breed a new race of journalists with a revived interest. Country Joe will be overjoyed at the presence of a journalist.'

'You mean they investigate extrasensory perception here?'

'You should know since they have sent you here to get a story,' the old man said. 'Still, most reporters don't have the foggiest idea what they're out to report, so you're excused.'

I hadn't any notion what the older man knew about the blue cat or where I stood in the general picture, except that he had nothing to do with the organizations out to get me. And his mischievous idea

I was a reporter might at least get me past the door to have a look around.

'So, ESP?' I said.

'Country Joe was most excited. So much so he didn't have time to tell me what it was all about, except they'd got amazing results this morning. So, I hurried over. ESP is about to go poof, so it's best to get it when it's hot. I have an agreement with Country Joe to call me over the moment anything flashes - thank God! - Country Joe isn't at all security-minded. So, you may get a real scoop, Mr...?'

'Tillet. Maurice Tillet.'

The old man's hand pressed with a feathery touch. 'Captain Trips.'

'Captain Trips...?'

'All in good time. Everything I've been telling you is top security, the death penalty and all. But I'm getting so senile I don't like security regulations. So I'm likely to babble anything. I keep telling Joe M. he'll have to have me taken care of someday.'

'Joe M.?'

Captain Trips made an apologetic grimace 'President McCarthy. But, of course, he was normal when I first met him, and now he's a besotted, scripture quoting barrel of insanity. So, I drop in on him now and again for a hoot. He's one of my pipelines to what's happening in the world, though the security services don't tell him too much these days. But that's where I learned about the blue cat.'

I was processing what I'd learned when I heard footsteps behind me.

The man who looked like a brother of Celeste was standing in the gateway. The mansion door opened, revealing a scholarly man whose face was twitching with excitement and nervousness. His coat had two bulging briefcase pockets, while they crammed his vest with enough micro books to make up a dozen encyclopaedias, plus two micro notebooks with a stylus and a fountain pen.

'Captain Trips!' he said in a high-pitched voice that expressed both fluster and delight. 'You've come at a fascinating moment!'

'That's the way I like them, Arthur,' said Captain Trips. 'Where's Country Joe?'

But Arthur was looking at me.

'Oh,' Captain Trips said, 'this is Maurice Tillet.' his eyes twinkled. 'Maurice Tillet, this is Arthur Brown.'

Arthur beamed at me as if I were a donor with a $100,000 check.

'This is most gratifying, Mr Tillet,' he said.

The man at the gate came clumping up behind us. I felt a gust of uneasiness, but the newcomer treated us all to a big, innocent grin that brought out all the handsomeness of his faun-like face.

'This is Cosmo.'

Arthur Brown was about to melt with gratification.

'Come in, come in, gentlemen,' he said. 'I'm sure you'll first want to tour our little establishment and have a peek at all our projects, and I'm sure you'll all want to go straight to Country Joe and get the full story. When he turns up, that is. I don't have the faintest idea of his whereabouts. Things have been popping everywhere since this morning. In every project. We'll have to tour the institute to find him.'

Captain Trips flashed me a look of humorous resignation. Cosmo pressed past me, sparking his wide white teeth at everyone and saying, 'Is fine, fine.' My spirits rose. I felt sure I was getting nearer to Zen.

XV

The Institute for Advanced Study was a gloomy Edwardian mansion grafted to a disorganized scientific enterprise. Small microfilm files elbowed glass shelves of leather-bound books that hadn't opened for decades. Blackened portraits of the institute founders looked down on machines and fluorescent screens blended with a dozen recordings of the brain waves. Drawing rooms that set one thinking of bustles and teacups instead held solemn-faced girls with electrodes attached to twenty parts of their bodies. Laboratory technicians in loose smocks caught their heels in stair carpets a hundred years old. But today, there was an excitement that pushed the Edwardian half of the place far into the background and brightened the grime on the walls. They did not even notice Arthur Brown and his little train of visitors.

Clairvoyants sketching objects being imagined by someone three floors away didn't look up from their blackboards. A technician darted out with a large syringe and took air samples under their noses without being aware of their presence. Correlating engines hummed and spat sparks. I was so busy peering about for the blue cat that I heard little of what Arthur Brown said. Instead, occasional, high-pitched descriptive phrases floated back to me 'telepathic communion with lower animals... shares the cells of an amoeba... No, I don't know where Country Joe is. I'm busy with important visitors... telekinesis will make television obsolete....'

Finally, plodding behind Cosmo up the stairs, Arthur Brown said. 'Now, I'm about to show you an experiment in telepathy that is underway. One day, it will be possible for two individuals to lay their minds side by side and compare all their feelings in the raw.'

'It's good!' Cosmo interjected.

Arthur Brown frowned at the interruption before remembering it was a journalist talking. He went on, 'In this case, we have only a preliminary stage: two individuals, using prolonged speech, writing, sketching, musical expression and so forth. They are attempting to share their innermost thoughts so much that they will become telepathic, as to be the case with husbands and wives.'

As they came to the top of the stairs, Arthur Brown continued a bit, 'the young man in this experiment is one of our most consistent performers, while the young lady is a volunteer who devotes her leisure time to science.'

He paused with his hand on an ancient brass doorknob.

'Let's not disturb them, Arthur,' Captain Trips suggested. 'Sounds like an intimate experiment.'

Arthur Brown shook his head. He opened the door, looked in, gasped, and slammed it - though not before Cosmo, peering over his shoulder, had emitted an appreciative and whinnying chortle.

'You're right, Captain Trips. We'd best not disturb them. Research is a strenuous affair.'

'Perfect!' Cosmo assured them. Arthur Brown looked at him, shook himself a bit and said, 'It now remains, gentlemen, to give you a glimpse of our crowning glory. If you'd like to follow me up this circular staircase….'

'I'll stay here, Arthur,' Captain Trips told him. 'Touring research can be strenuous.'

'But I imagine Country Joe must be on the roof.'

'Bring him down.'

As I trudged up the musty cylinder lit by the tiny bullseye windows, my feet clanking on worn metal treads, it occurred to me that Zen seemed to have been having a field day here, bringing people together in love and understanding and whatnot. It made me jealous of the way Zen was strewing his favours around.

From behind, Arthur Brown's voice filtered up. 'I should preface this ascent by saying that one of the institute's chief motives is the conviction that humanity will soon destroy itself unless superior power intervenes. So, we are bound to apply what little knowledge of ESP we have gained to seeking such intervention. Even if there is only one chance in a million of contacting a superior power where the stakes are so great in the universe, we must not overlook the chance. So, gentlemen, please watch out for the next-to-last step. There isn't any.'

I was just putting my foot on it and caught myself. So I took a bigger step, and I was out on the roof and under the saucer in the next moment.

Arthur Brown handed out dark glasses and urged Cosmo and me up a ladder that led to a small platform next to the saucer's rim. The interior shone so much that I clamped my eyes shut and put on the black glasses.

'The exact nature of waves is unknown,' said Arthur. 'They move at least at speeds far greater than light. We have yet to get a figure on them. But we have timed thought-casts between here and New Zealand - the human or physiological factor confounds us. They may not be waves at all. They may reflect and refract like light.'

'Is right,' interjected Cosmo.

'You think so?' Arthur Brown questioned.

La Prensa's faun-like representative shrugged his muscular shoulders.

'Just guessing,' he said.

'At any rate,' Arthur Brown continued. 'We are working on that latter supposition here. This copper structure is a parabolic mirror. The waves were originating at its focus, concentrating into a beam directed into the sky toward any stellar, planetary systems.'

'Amazing,' Cosmo grunted. 'Explains everything.'

'What do you mean?' Arthur Brown.

'I am humble before the world of science,' Cosmo told him.

Arthur Brown frowned. 'One day, the message now being beamed, with its appeal for help from war-threatened and deluded humanity, may reach a mature and benign race, which will come to our aid? '

I studied the gleaming saucer through my dark glasses, and it became less of a jumble of highlights. Projecting from a hole in the centre of the bowl was a brownish-red blob wearing goggles that looked as if made of a darker glass than my specs. The blob's lips moved.

S-O-S, from planet earth. S-O-S, from planet earth.'

'That is our star broadcaster of ESP,' Arthur Brown laughed, 'if you'll pardon a pun of which we're fond. To be sure, it's thought waves, not sound waves. He's originating, but it helps him ESP if he says the message. He's a bit of an eccentric - a monk - but religion is a common theme with most of our best people.'

I saw that the sweating head at the focus of the parabolic mirror was that of the monk I knew. The monk saw me and disappeared from the saucer.

'He shouldn't do that,' Arthur Brown said. 'There's at least twenty minutes of his shift remaining. Well, I presume you've seen all you need for your articles, gentlemen. We'd best go down.'

As my foot touched the roof, the monk darted up to me, sweat pouring off his ruddy-bronze forehead.

'What are you doing here?' he said.

'The critical point,' said the monk. 'Is that *he's* here, isn't he? The Blue One!'

Before I could answer, Arthur Brown and Cosmo glanced at us. The monk and I followed them down the metal staircase. We found Captain Trips deep in conversation with a man who looked at least half out of this world on the top floor. He was plump and had a beard, but his eyes seemed to see twice as much as he was looking at.

The monk tugged at my sleeve. 'That's Country Joe,' he whispered, his lips next to my ear.

'But can you explain it, Country Joe?' Captain Trips was saying.

'Why all this sudden success with ESP in all your projects?'

Country Joe frowned. 'Well, there is one unusual circumstance, man. Our lab technicians have found a sort of specialized protein waking up.'

'Do you mean to suggest that this creature handles the ESP results we've been getting?'

Country Joe did. 'I do,' he said.

'But, why?'

'I don't know what I've been making of those farfetched guesses.'

'Guesses!'

'Well, we'll soon find out,' said Country Joe. He stepped past us toward the front end of the hall. His feet were stirring dust from the ancient carpet. 'We'll have a look at this animal and see what we think about it. Dr Sakura!' he called.

Country Joe's face went a little further out of the world. 'They all do. everybody at the Foundation.'

The door opened at the front end of the hall, and a long-nosed young lady in a lab smock stepped out.

'Would you care to see this blue animal with your outer eyes?' she said.

'We sure would, Doc,' said Country Joe.

I wanted to burst out with all my information about Zen, but Cosmo forestalled me. 'Gentlemen,' he said. 'Best to tell you now....'

Zen strode out of the door from which Dr Sakura had emerged. He strode like a self-confident blue god. The long-nosed girl closed the door.

The monk squeezed my upper arm and a voice came from behind.

'Break to either side, everybody.'

Special Agent Stone was standing at the head of the stairs. The representative of the FBI was looking both knowledgeable and competent, though even more grey-haired and anxious than the last time I'd seen him.

He levelled his stun gun and punched the trigger. But his nerves couldn't have been good as they were, for instead of the blue cat collapsing, Dr Sakura pitched over on her face, gasping.

'My nose - I can't see it!'

Special Agent Stone grimaced and re-directed his stun-gun as the dust mushroomed up from the carpet around Dr Sakura. Then, suddenly, he felt the golden wave billowing out from Zen.

Stone's face turned red, and his fingers uncurled from the gun as if invisible hands were prying them away. It dropped to the floor. Another voice behind us, languid and scornful, said, 'Stay where you are, gentlemen. It would be dangerous to move your hands.'

Pandora wore a grey dress, and a large handbag swung from her shoulder. She stood at the head of the stairs looking even more beautiful than the last time I saw her. In her slender hand was a big gun.

A vague memory nagged at me. She couldn't hurt anyone while Zen was there. Meanwhile, the violet blonde was walking forward in a business-like way. She didn't even glance at Cosmo. As she passed Special Agent Stone, her free hand snatched the stun-gun, grabbed at a larger one inside his coat, then dropped them both in her handbag, and kept going straight for the cat. Now she'll get it, I told myself. But she kept straight on - Zen seemed to study her. He sprang back onto the windowsill, his blue fur rose, his muzzle lengthened, and out came a prolonged, spitting hiss.

The next moment I felt such a formless terror as I had never known. As if all reality were about to be crunched in a single fist. As if the blackness between the stars were lashing down to strangle me. I gazed at Zen as if the blue cat had turned into a devil. Pandora stooped to grab him. The cat streaked past her, but Pandora's hands were faster. The cat sprang straight at her face, claws raking, but Pandora detached him and shoved him in her handbag and shut it. She looked as beautiful and composed as she had at the stairhead. No blood flowed from the scratches on her face. As she passed Cosmo, he looked up at her.

'You jerk,' she said to him and walked on and went down the stairs.

I felt my heart hammering ten, eleven, twelve times, like a clock striking. Then I was racing downstairs, and someone was pounding down after me. I darted through the open front door and stumbled down the steps in time to see a dark car roar off.

Special Agent Stone was beside me now, barking orders into a pocket radio. From the other end of the street, another car shot in. Red plumes shot forward from under its hood as it rocket-braked to a heaving stop. Stone piled into the back seat. I scrambled in after him.

'You can still see them,' Stone yelled at the driver. 'Rockets!' he turned to me. 'Who are you?'

'Maurice Tillet,' I said, 'I'm a journalist!' but the reply disappeared in the rocket's roar.

The other car had been about five blocks away when we had taken off. As I untwisted myself with difficulty from the huddle into which acceleration had thrown me, I saw it had reduced its lead to one block.

'Douse the jets,' Stone ordered. 'We can curb them on our regulars but watch they don't shift. They may have rocketed. Where do you stand in Project Kitty, Tillet?'

'As a special observer,' I improvised, still hanging on with both hands. 'My section has decided the blue cat may not be dangerous.'

'What?' Stone demanded, peering ahead.

'Didn't you see it up there?'

'What?' Stone said, his eyes measuring the lessening distance between the two cars. 'You mean the horror?'

'No,' I said. 'The peaceful feeling!'

The car ahead of us slowed a bit, and something blue flashed out of it, roiled over half a dozen times, and darted toward an alley.

'Brakes!' Stone yelled, and I tumbled into the lap of the man beside the driver as the forward rockets jetted and the back of the car lifted and slammed down. I realised I was the only one left in the car and scrambled out.

'The alley's blind; there's no way for it to get out,' said Stone. 'Advance abreast. Tillet, back us up!'

'Don't hurt him,' I warned.

'We know enough for that!' Stone yelled back.

I was behind them by this time and saw the blue cat crouching in the narrow alley's blind end, twenty feet away from the advancing men. The distance lessened to ten, and the blue cat darted forward, dodged this way, that, and dove between Stone and the man to my right, straight into my outstretched hands.

'Zen!' I said, lifting the cat closer. Five claws raked my chin while fifteen others dug into my hands. I looked at the little face. Except for its colour, it was an ordinary, spitting, angry cat face. I could smell the blue dye.

'Here,' I said and tossed the animal to Stone. 'It's a fake! They had it all ready and threw it out to misdirect us.'

Stone sprinted to the car. But I was not with him. I hadn't the heart. So as the rockets roared again, I stood halfway down the alley, scratched and weary.

XVI

The elevator door closed behind me, and I started the weary climb from twenty-eight to twenty-nine. I had set forth from my room to look at life and plunge into an adventure. And it had happened. I had seen much of life and been buffeted by vast oceans of experience. My brain still buzzed from it. Yet, during those incredible twenty-four hours, it had seemed to me my whole character was changing. I was becoming the daring yet sympathetic adventurer I had always dreamed of being.

Yet there I was, dragging myself back to my room, having pulled my usual trick of saying 'No,' when I wanted, to say 'Yes.' from the speed with which I was falling back into my old habits, I knew I'd spend the evening spying on Ms Celeste from my darkened window. Oh, I could tell myself there was no reason to give a second to a pretty ordinary woman when I'd met such a desirable girl as Judy Womack and seen such a beauty as Pandora, not to mention sharing the society of such grotesque but attractive characters Cleopatra Jones and the nun. But it was rationalization, and I knew it. This world was more my size.

I could once more tell myself that I would be brave and bold again if only Zen were at my side. But even that was no longer true. The fact was everything had become much too big for me. I wanted the blue cat, yes, but I wanted him as my special pet, my mascot, my good luck cat, something to sleep at the foot of the bed - not a mysterious mutant monster that kept getting me involved with male and female wrestlers, religious crackpots, gun-toting psychoanalysts, girls with claws, revolutionaries, hippy scientists, ESP senders, syndicates, FBI raids, national and international crimes, and a lot of other things that were much, much too big for me.

I coded open my door, stepped inside, and had closed it behind me when I realised I was not returning to loneliness just yet.

On her hands and knees, looking under my bed, but now with her face turned towards me, was the black-haired, faun-like girl whose window was opposite me. I froze in every muscle, my hand locked to the ajar door, ready to jerk it open and run.

'Celeste?'

She got up with a smile. 'Hello,' she said in a warm voice with a foreign accent I couldn't place. 'I have lost something. Maybe it hides in here.' She smoothed out the black, grey suit I'd watched her take off last night. She ran her hand back across her head and down the ponytail in which her hair-do ended.

'Something?' I said, my hand still glued fast behind me. I couldn't help it, but every time I looked her in the eye, my gaze had to travel down her figure to her 10-inch platform shoes.

'Yes,' she confirmed, 'a - you call him - a pussycat.', after a bit, her smile widened, and she shook a finger at me. "Have you peek at me, you naughty boy?'

I gulped and said nothing, but her remark did a great deal to humanize her for me. Hallucinations don't typically make me blush.

'It's all right,' she said. 'Windows across, why not? Same thing - windows across and both open a little - make me think that maybe my pussycat jumps over here. So, I step across to see.'

'Step across?' I bit my lip, my gaze once more shooting to her legs.

'Sure,' she said and showed the window. 'Look.'

With considerable reluctance, I unstuck my hand from the door and walked to the open window. Spanning the ten feet between it and the opposite was a flimsy-looking telescope ladder of grey metal.

I turned around. 'Is it a blue cat you're looking for?'

Her face brightened. 'So, Bastet the Powerful did jump across.'

'Who?'

'Bastet the Powerful - it's the name of a pussycat, though he much more than that.'

'I called him Zen,'

'What is this Zen? A famous general.'

'Not quite. By the way, I think I met your brother today, a journalist named Cosmo, representing the newspaper *La Prensa*.'

'That's right,' she said. 'Please, where my brother and pussycat now?'

'I don't have the faintest idea,' I said.

'It's nothing new. We are crazy people, always lose each other.'

'I can't place your accent,' I said. 'Where are you from, France?'

'Sure,' she said, her eyes darting.

'Tell me, Celeste,' I went on. 'Does your cat have peculiar powers over people?'

She frowned at me. 'Peculiar powers?'

'I mean, can he make people happy?'

The frown smoothed. 'Sure. Nice little pussycat, make people happy!'

Once again, I couldn't keep my gaze from flickering to her legs.

'Celeste,' I said. 'I've got a lot more questions for you, but I don't think you know English well enough to answer them. But maybe if I tell you what's been happening to me, you'll be able to. At least, I hope so. It's a long, long story.'

'Excellent idea,' she agreed, sinking on the bed.

I placed myself in the foam chair opposite, and for the next hour, I told her the story of what had happened ever since I had found Zen sitting on the windowsill.

I suppressed the incident of watching her through the portal, which made it necessary for me to condense the account of my session with Dr Womack. Celeste often interrupted to ask for explanations, obvious things, such as a hatpin, the Federal Bureau of Investigation, or what male and female wrestlers tried to do to each other in the ring? She passed up some things I expected to puzzle her, though I couldn't always tell whether this was because she understood them or because she didn't want to. Her usual comment was along these lines: 'That blue pussycat is so stupid. But Zen, that's a good name you give him.'

When I came to the Institute for Advanced Study and her brother, she rolled over on her stomach and listened with closer attention. But when I mentioned Cosmo had seemed to develop such an instant yen for Pandora, she whooped. 'Oh, my brother. He chases anything with two legs and milk glands. Unless he is pregnant.'

'What!'

'Did I say something? Must use the wrong word,' Celeste interposed, brushing the matter off.

But she was interested in Captain Trips and insisted on me telling her a great deal about him.

'He smart man,' she said with conviction. 'Very much like meet.'

'I'll try to manage it next time,' I said and told her how Pandora had captured the blue cat.

Celeste shook her head. 'People got tough hearts,' she said.

I rounded off my story to account for the fake blue cat in the alley that had scratched me. She reached over and touched my hands. 'Poor Maurice,' she said. 'We know who have pussycat, but not where?'

'That's right,' I said. 'And where is tough because Mr Brimstone is hiding from the FBI?'

I stood, trying not to make it clear I wanted to put a few feet between us. Celeste's fingers were soft enough, but there was something about her touch and her close presence that set me shivering. It was her odour, which wasn't strong or even unpleasant. She didn't smell of anything at all.

'Well, that's my story, Celeste,' I said. 'And now I want to ask my questions. What kind of cat have you got that Love Incorporated could hope to bribe the federal government with a mutant with telepathic powers that can control emotions?'

But instead of answering me, she smiled and said, 'Excuse me, but a long story. Be right back.'

I expected her to walk out the window and wondered what I'd do if she did. But she went into the bathroom and shut the door.

I paced around, lifting small objects, and putting them down again. I turned on the TV to distract myself but didn't look at it. Then, on the following circuit of the room, I trod hard when I passed the TV, and something went wrong with it. The sound sank to a low mumble, and I was once more alone in my agitation.

So much so I jumped when I heard a slight noise behind me.

The hall door had opened. Judy Womack was standing outside, looking both adolescent and weary in a faded blue sweater and slacks. A lock of her long, dark hair trailed in front of her ear. She fixed on me with a defiant stare.

'Last night I said, goodbye forever, and I meant it. So don't get any ideas. I've come here to warn you about something.' Her voice broke a little. 'Not that Ralf, Florian, and Wolfgang hate me, or you tried to make me get mushy and humble. When I came home by the service chute early this morning, I overheard my father talking with two other men. I found out he's a Chinese agent, and his job is to get the blue cat no matter how much killing it takes. And he thinks you have it.'

I looked at her, and the hours between vanished. I was back in the little tangled square at dawn, and Judy was about to leave me, and all my snapping nervous tension flowed in a new and steadier channel.

'I wasn't trying to humble you,' I said.

'Oh?' she said, tucking the lock of hair back of her ear.

I moved closer. 'I was conceited and jealous.'

'Be careful what you say, Maurice,' she whispered.

'All right,' I said. 'I was trying to humble you; I was doing my best to. But unfortunately, I was full of the sort of vanity and condescension that comes from overthinking. I didn't know if your sort of defiance and glory has a place in the world, Judy, but I love you.'

I put my arms around her, and she didn't vanish. The feeling of her body against me wasn't like any something I'd imagined. It was trusting and exhausted. Her chin lifted from my shoulder, and she shoved me back about six feet. She was glaring at and beyond me. It relieved me she didn't have a gun or claws.

Celeste leaned against the bathroom door, watching us. 'Hello,' she said. 'Girlfriend?'

Judy turned pale. 'How many do you try to take on at once?' she said.

'Don't worry,' said Celeste. 'He timid at first.'

'Good to know,' mumbled Judy.

The TV came on loud again.

'... it's been long suspected that Cleopatra and her husband weren't on sleeping terms. But her fans had to wait until what, with the outlawing of male-female wrestling, was her last professional appearance before getting a glimpse of her new boyfriend.'

In the middle of the bright screen was me, with a dazed look and a silly smile on my face. Cleopatra's arm clutched around me.

Judy crashed her palm against my left cheek. Then, she ran out the door and slammed it behind her. I stood there for a few seconds. Then I turned off the TV.

'Why you no chase?' Celeste inquired. 'Don't worry. She comes back. She loves you even more. She proud you such a virile man, have many girls.'

'Please,' I groaned, lifting my hand. 'I'm pretty sure that was goodbye forever.'

'Forever is never. She comes back,' Celeste said.

There was a timid knock at the door. I opened it. Dr Womack pointed at my neck with a stun gun and walked in. The small psychoanalyst looked professional in the old-fashioned business suit, white shirt and necktie affected by doctors. There was even a vest buttoned over his slight paunch. His left cheek was smooth, as his gleaming bald head; he'd covered the scratches with skin film. His expression radiated fatherly goodwill, though he kept the stun-gun pointed straight at me. Now and then, his gaze flickered to Celeste.

'I won't deny the statement my daughter made about me. Who could know but you, Maurice, how psychotic civilization has become? But, of course, I should have said all this last night and appealed to your reason.'

He kept the stun-gun trained on my neck with geometric precision. 'But I was hurried and upset - even our agents are not immune to the infection when living with it and I made several mistakes. I did not take my unfortunate daughter into account early enough, though I am glad she came to warn you since it enabled me to find you. Which will enable you and your charming companion to enjoy the bracing sanity of the Chinese Secret Service.'

The small psychiatrist smiled and propped himself on the arm of the foam chair.

'And now, children,' he said. 'I am going to tell you how you can do a great service to the nation and win an undying welcome whenever you visit China.'

'What do you want the blue cat for?' I said.

'It is my firm belief that blue cats are ordinary cats with tiny electronic transmitters inserted into their bodies and with hormone spraying capacities comparable to those of skunks,' said Dr Womack. 'The blue cats are the most important element in a planned assault on the Chinese psyche. But unfortunately, we could not lay our hands on one of these creatures to confirm our deductions and shape proper countermeasures. We must do so now.'

'But there's only one blue cat,' I said.

'I am giving you the facts,' Dr Womack assured me. 'Those stories you have heard are blinds put up by the capitalist government to conceal from its slaves and pseudo-scientists the enormity of its actions. What has happened is a blue cat has escaped from a government laboratory. You led me to that cat once, Maurice. You can do it again.'

'I can't,' I said.

'You can.'

'Last time you had him; all you did was let him go again.'

For the first time, a shadow of impatience darkened Dr Womack's geniality. 'I told you I made mistakes. It was all I could do to escape the FBI raid. But it won't happen again.' His voice grew brisk. 'So come along Maurice and bring your friend. There's no more time for discussion.'

'But...'

Celeste stepped into the foreground. 'I do not go,' she said. 'Why should I? You sound crazy head!'

The psychoanalyst lifted his eyebrows. 'I was about to take up your case, young lady. Why are you here in the first place?'

'Come from the room across,' Celeste told him, jerking a thumb at the window.

'So, you're the young lady Mr Tillet watched undressing last night. I thought you were a delusion.'

'Maurice, you never tell me about that,' said Celeste.

'He wouldn't!'

'Why not? I don't care. If Maurice like it, it's okay.'

'So, you're a common exhibitionist,' said Dr Womack. 'I see.'

Celeste planted her hands on her hips. 'I no say long words well. But you diagnose wrong there. Not exhibition.' And she peeled off a stocking. I watched in fascinated horror.

Womack stood up. 'If you are trying to appeal to my...'

Celeste pulled off her shoe and foot and held out her dainty black hoof, fur-tufted fetlock, and slim pastern for Dr Womack's inspection. 'Okay, she said. 'Inspect!'

Dr Womack's knees shook his face grey. Then, without warning, Celeste stooped, spun around, and let go with a powerful kick.

The stun-gun shot out of Womack's trembling hand and clattered against the wall. The Dr snatched his hand away and stumbled out of the room. His rapid, uneven footsteps faded out. I knew how he felt. It was all I could do not to follow him.

Celeste laughed, hobbled over to the door, and shut it. Then, she picked up Womack's gun.

I clutched at the table for support. 'Celeste,' I said, my teeth chattering. 'I think you come from a lot farther away than France.'

'Yes,' she said. 'I got a longer story than yours to tell.'

'But first if you please ...' I faltered and pointed at the shoe, foot, and crumpled stocking she'd dropped on the floor.

'Okay, Maurice.' She picked them up and sat on the edge of the bed to put them on. I followed her movements, but when she was about to thrust her hoof into the deep well in the wrong foot and the platform, I cringed and looked away.

'You got an idea where pussycat is?' she said.

'No, but I know where we might find out.'

'Is in this city?'

'Yes.'

'You take me there, Maurice?'

'I guess so.'

'Don't you want to find pussycat too?'

'Yes.'

I forced myself to steal a glance at her and let out a sigh of relief. Her two legs were once more like any other girl's. Illusion, I decided, was the Bread of Life.

'Now you can answer those questions of mine, celeste.'

But there was more rapping at the door.

'This time, girlfriend,' said Celeste.

But I was taking no more chances. I switched on the one-way peephole first and looked straight into the face of Special Agent Stone.

When I whispered, 'FBI,' to Celeste, she jumped up. During my lengthy narrative, she'd asked several questions about the organization. I had answered them, and she had formed definite conclusions. 'We got to go, Maurice! No time question-answer now.' she sprang to the windowsill and across the ladder.

It wasn't as long as the temple's beam, but it was ten times higher, and I wasn't drunk. If I hadn't crossed the beam at the temple and gone down the service chute at the Womack's', I would never have dared it. My heart was hammering as I stepped down into Celeste's room. I turned around with a vague idea of removing the ladder. But, instead, I heard a crash. Celeste grabbed me.

'No time now,' she said.

Seconds later, we were entering the elevator on her side of the building. 'That's the up button,' I warned as she punched it.

'I know, I know,' she said.

Emerging onto the roof brought an immense sense of freedom. The sun had not set, and everything around us was bright. I saw a half dozen copters swinging in low toward us like bugs. Celeste was hustling me along toward an empty corner of the roof. Then, a mighty voice from the sky commanded us to stop.

Celeste halted at the edge of the roof, fell around, climbed a couple of feet up and stood there. She opened in the air a small doorway and climbed inside. She turned around, her face a pale mask in an inky rectangle.

'Come on, Maurice,' she said and stretched a white arm out of the rectangle down toward me.

I stared at this weird air-framed portrait. Beneath me, it was the sheer walls of the building opposite and the dizzying ribbon of the street fifty floors below. Then, behind me, men shouted, and there was another shattering command from the sky.

'Stop what you are doing and give yourselves up!'

I grabbed Celeste's wrist. My other hand, fumbling, found an invisible rung in the air. So did my foot. I scrambled up and pitched over the threshold of the inky doorway and found a curving floor under me. Rolling over, I saw behind me a rectangle of the sky with three stars in it. The rectangle narrowed and vanished, and there was no light at all.

Then, I fell.

XVII

How long would it take a man to fall fifty floors? I vomited but brought up only the ghosts of a yeast-spread sandwich and a glass of soybean milk consumed a day before.

I continued to fall.

Soft light sprang up around me, and I discovered I was inside a sphere eight feet in diameter. Swivelling my gaze past my feet, I noticed Celeste sprawled in the air studying a screen set in the sphere's lining.

But I was still falling.

I knew little about spaceships, but I knew they couldn't go into free-fall without accelerating first to get a kind of edge on earth's gravitational field.

But there had been no acceleration.

'Celeste!' I yelled, which in the confined space was deafening. 'What's happening to me?'

Wincing a bit, she looked around at me. 'Shh, Maurice. You in free-fall but not falling. I turn off gravity.'

Still retching, I tried to comprehend the idea. 'Turn off gravity?' I was still falling but no longer so sure I was going to hit anything.

Celeste looked along my sprawling body at my face. 'Sure. Gravity goes around this little boat as light does. Gravity no pulls it, light does.'

'That's why it was invisible?'

'Wait a bit, I, got do something...'

'But in a ship like this, you could travel!'

'This does not ship, is a dinghy. No talk now.'

My falling gained a new direction. I drifted toward Celeste.

'Here beside me, Maurice,' she instructed.

A short while later, I was on my stomach beside Celeste, my head poised like hers above the screen. And the speed of my newly directed fall increased, although the sphere was no longer falling with me until I pressed my body against the soft lining. I tried to look at the screen. At first, I couldn't interpret the picture. It was in shades of violet and showed a few large squares and oblongs with dark ribbons between most of them. On the central square were several dots, which moved as I watched them were three or four crosses with blobs at their centres. The squares and rectangles shrank, while more of the same came onto the screen from the edges. I was looking down at the city, and the dots were the men hunting us, while the crosses were the copters.

My stomach chilled at the prospect of being poised so high above the city and going higher. But I lost myself in the pictures. I hadn't travelled a great deal by air and had seen even less when I'd done so that the growing image of the city was enthralling. I felt like a god.

'We are soon high enough, Maurice,' said Celeste. 'Hold on hands, stick feet under the bar.'

I obeyed her instructions, holding two handles and thrusting my legs under a large, padded bar. Again, I deduced we were decelerating. After a while, this stopped too, and I was once more 'in freefall but not falling.' Meanwhile, the picture on the screen had become one of the entire city—a checkerboard of tiny squares like a map.

Celeste unfolded an ordinary street map and flattened it out beside the screen.

'You say you know where to find pussycat?'

My first realization was flimsy. It depended on Mr Brimstone having the blue cat, Hercules Jones knowing where Mr Brimstone was hiding from the FBI, and Hercules hiding at the temple. Still, it was the only way of finding Zen.

It occurred to me I didn't know where the temple was located. But a memory of a vast shop window full of marching mannequins came to my rescue. The temple was next to Monster Multi-Products, and everybody knew where that was. So, I found it for Celeste on the street map and the screen. Soon we were speeding upward, so I had to cling to the handles again while the squares on the net grew larger, with Monster Multi-Products moving toward the centre.

I asked Celeste to answer the questions I'd put to her in my room, but she cut me off with, 'No time now. But, first, find pussycat.'

Our descent slowed. Celeste manoeuvred the dinghy around Monster Multi-Products until I spotted, at the base of the building next to it, the tiny slot showing the cubical pocket of space in which the temple stood robbed of its air-rights.

As we dropped into the canyon of the street past windowed and windowless walls, I could make out beetles and tinier bugs - cars and people. Soon we were hovering only ten feet above the sidewalk and the unsuspecting pedestrians.

Celeste slipped the dinghy between the rail of the sidewalk and the 'floor' of the tall building over the temple. The picture grew dark. We descended a little farther, past the top-level street and the one next below it, until we were a couple of feet above the pile of bricks from the fallen chimney. Celeste moved controls. The screen went blank, the lights went out, and with breath-taking suddenness, my body crunched into the soft lining as my weight returned.

'Got legs down for the dinghy to stand on,' Celeste told me. 'Quiet now, Maurice.'

A slit of lesser darkness appeared beyond Celeste. It widened to a rectangle through which I could make out a section of the temple porch. The rectangle was obstructed. Celeste climbed out through it. I followed her, feet first, moving them around until they found the rungs, and climbed down until I could step off onto the temple's gritty front yard. I looked up. As far as I could see, there was nothing above me except the two upper-level streets and the dull black 'ceiling' above the house.

'All safe,' Celeste assured me. 'Nobody climbs over rocks, bump in ladder legs. This place, Maurice?'

The temple looked more ancient and worn than ever. A gaping wound was in the two upper stories, and the occupants had done nothing to bandage it. A little light glowed through the shutters of the living-room windows. Stepping, with an eye, cocked on the slanting wall, I led Celeste up onto the porch and around the corner. I hesitated in front of the old door with the tiny cat door cut in the bottom, lifted my hand to the cat-headed knocker and banged it twice. After a while, there were footsteps, the old-style peephole was open, and this time I recognised the monk's watery eye.

'Greetings, Maurice,' said the latter. 'Who is that with you?'

'A young lady named Celeste.'

The monk opened the door. 'Fate must be at work. Her brother's here.'

XVIII

The monk's altar for Zen consisted of a small table set against the far wall and covered with red velvet trailed to the floor in graceful folds. He'd fastened it to the wall above an ancient crux ansata, the Egyptian cross with looped top, symbolizing procreation and life. On lower tables to either side were large unlit candles and statuettes of Egyptian gods: Isis, whip-wielding Osiris, and cat-headed Bastet itself.

There was the same profusion of cats, though they were no longer as peaceful as they'd been when Zen was in the house. They tramped about with ears drawn back and fur fluffed; they ambushed each other from behind and under furniture; they snarled and jumped whenever they met. Those wolfing the bits of food left on plates would lift their heads every few seconds to hiss warnings. The only one asleep was curled on Zen's altar.

They placed a low dark table inlaid with a silver pentacle in the centre of the room. Beside it sat Cleopatra Jones, still in her shabby Egyptian dress with the ripped sleeves hanging from her meaty arms, but with her flower-covered hat once more jammed down over her cropped blonde hair. She looked sullen and on the defensive.

Across the table from her, leaning forward in their chairs, sat Cosmo and Captain Trips. Both stood. The monk swept Celeste and me into the room, saying, 'Our council of war - or I should say muscular peace - is complete!'

Captain Trips smiled, his mind hungry for all facts. He liked a grubby bohemian atmosphere. Cosmo spotted Celeste, put down an enormous glass of whiskey and whooped out three or four words in a foreign language. Then, finally, he caught himself and changed to, 'Hello, darling sister! Great to see you.'

He hugged her with a hungriness that struck me as odd. She wasn't too sisterly about it herself.

'That's 'enough,' she told him. 'Great, see you too, dumbhead. About time turn up.'

Cosmo looked hurt until he got to his glass of whiskey. 'Now what was I doing?' he said.

'Getting drunk?' she said.

'Not drunk!' The excitement got the better of him again, and he burst out with, 'We finding pussycat!'

There was a giggle I recognized. Looking around, I saw the nun sitting in her nook, backed by her shelves of wax dolls and busy at work sewing clothes for another under a large magnifier. She had shifted to an off-the-bosom evening dress and tied a vast blue bow around her coarse dark hair.

'That French guy, he cracks me up in little pieces every time he says a word,' she gurgled, without pausing in her work. 'He's so adorable.'

'Thanks, sweetheart,' Cosmo, waving his glass at her, 'I adorable all over.'

Celeste suppressed a laugh and whispered to me. 'I told you: two legs and milk glands.'

The monk ignored the flirtatious interchange. Instead, his sun-burned features gleamed with controlled excitement. 'This young lady is Celeste. She is Cosmo's sister,' he told Captain Trips and Cleopatra. He turned to me. 'I suppose you're wondering why Captain Trips and Cosmo are here? I brought them along with me from the institute because both of them are interested in *him*. Among the lot of us, we have an excellent chance of delivering *him* from his enemies.'

'What means, him?' said Celeste. 'You mean pussycat?'

'I mean the Blue One,' The monk confirmed. 'I mean Bastet Returned, the Bringer of Love.'

Celeste didn't bother with that. 'Introduce me to Captain Trips, please,' she whispered.

I performed the desired introduction.

Captain Trips surprised me by kissing Celeste's hand and not letting go of it. He didn't behave at all like a scientist of eighty-plus years should. And Celeste turned on a lot more charm than I recalled her using on me. The two of them stood there murmuring intelligent nothings to each other. I felt a jealous impulse to call out to Captain Trips, 'Wait until you see her real legs.' Still, I suspected Captain Trips wouldn't be shocked at Celeste's real legs or anything about her. Instead, I had noted a lack of surprise come into Captain Trips' face. He took her hand with eager interest.

His voice became sharp, clear, and romantic: 'Delighted to meet you, Celeste.'

She turned to the others with a self-satisfied smile. 'Captain and I got much to talk about,' she announced. 'Excuse me, please. Cosmo, you take care of pussycat business.'

Celeste and Captain Trips strolled out through the room arm in arm, beaming at each other and chatting like old friends.

'They don't have any great regard for the importance of the situation,' said the monk. 'So, we'll carry on by ourselves, making plans to rescue the Blue One. Mr Tillet, what have you to contribute?'

I told them how I'd found Zen at Love Incorporated, lost him again, and then caught up with him before Pandora grabbed him at the Institute for Advanced Study.

As soon as I finished, the nun cut in. She was sewing clothes and put them on a bulky doll that I recognized as the Mr Treacle she'd worked on before. To my amazement, she was even putting underwear on the doll and slipping tiny objects into its pants pockets with a pair of tweezers.

'Did you find out why Dr Womack kidnapped those three cats of ours?' she said.

I explained, as best as I could, what had happened to them.

The nun looked over her shoulder and got the doll that was the image of Dr Womack and fixed on it her most witchy stare.

'Slow, slow acid dripped on your forehead,' she incanted with a sincerity that sent gooseflesh coursing under my shirt. 'And I hope days before it gets in your eye. That's the first and mildest of your torments.'

 Then, she picked up the doll she'd been dressing and told it, 'That goes for you as well.'

A sudden catfight prevented me from finding out how nasty the nun's imagination could get. The monk separated the five squalling felines with a few painless but strategic kicks. Then, he hitched up his turquoise slacks and said, looking at the nun, 'Now we can forget all the hate and other dark vibrations and get down to business. Here's the situation, Mr Tillet. Earlier today, Cleopatra overheard her husband Hercules tell Virgil where Mr Brimstone and Mr Treacle are hiding. Now Hercules and Virgil are asleep upstairs....'

'Yes,' Cleopatra butted in. 'But they will not stay that way too much longer.'

'Not after what you put in their whiskey.' The monk thanked her with a thin smile. 'And, if they do wake up, I'm sure you can take care of the two of them. So, there's the situation, Mr Tillet. The only trouble is Cleopatra won't tell us where Mr Treacle is. We've pleaded with her, we've implored her, we've promised her things. I've done my best to explain to her the importance for the Blue One to be worshipped so that he will change the world. Cosmo flattered and jollied her, and Captain Trips was friendly. But she won't talk.'

'I won't talk to nuts like you,' the female wrestler told him. 'I'm not the sort of person who likes to be jollied!'

'Excuse, please,' Cosmo interrupted. 'What jollied mean?'

'And I don't enjoy the crazy talk,' Cleopatra said to the monk, ignoring Cosmo.

'Every reason you gave me for talking made me much surer I wouldn't.' She took a drink and turned toward me, her elbows on her large knees. 'Now, with you, it's different,' she said. 'I got to admit you're a daring little guy. I saw you go up against Mr Treacle, and from what I hear, you did more of the same later.'

'I just want to find the blue cat,' I said.

'That settles it for me. It's your cat, and you got a right to know where it is even if you get killed trying to get it. So, you want me to tell you in private or out in front of all these nutters?'

'Thank you, Cleo,' I whispered. 'Say it right out.'

Cleopatra opened her mouth and said, 'Oh, Lord.'

I turned around. Hercules and Virgil were coming in from the hall.

'Fine sort of wife you turned out to be,' said Hercules, striding toward Cleopatra with his hands shoved deep in his pockets. 'Can't leave you ten minutes before you pull a dumb trick like this.' With circles under his eyes and a day's beard growth, the little wrestler did a fair job of looking outraged and discouraged. But Virgil, imitating his hero, could produce only an expression like a baby about to cry.

'Getting sneaky, too,' Hercules observed. 'Spying on me.'

'Underhanded,' Virgil commented.

'Underhanded?' Cleopatra banged the silver table so hard it jumped, and she had to grab at her glass and the bottle. 'You two are underhanded!'

'I don't like the company you keep,' Hercules continued. 'That wimp was bad enough,' he said, giving me the barest glance before going on to Cosmo. 'But where between here and Pluto did you ever pick up this corny French gigolo.'

'Corny French gigolo,' Virgil added.

Cosmo, who had seemed uninterested, put down his glass and flew at Hercules. 'I don't like you,' he asserted. 'You want a kick in the face?'

'Do you know who you're talking to?' said Virgil.

'Don't fight, boys!' the nun called from the alcove. 'At least until I've finished this.' She was putting finishing touches on Mr Treacle's face under the magnifier.

'Don't worry,' said Hercules. 'I'm not looking for a fight. I'm too upset about this uneducated wife of mine.'

'Uneducated?' Cleopatra exploded. 'Well, I know where to find Mr Treacle, Mr Brimstone and the cat. So, you can stick that up to your arse.'

Hercules whirled toward her. 'You don't know what you're saying.'

'I don't know what I'm saying!' Cleopatra mocked. 'Listen up, Maurice. Mr Treacle is....'

'Cleopatra!' said Hercules yelled. 'Ten million dollars are riding on this deal. so long as Mr Brimstone has the blue cat to trade to the government.'

Cleopatra stared at him. For a second or two, there was silence.

The monk coughed.

'Hercules,' he said, 'I am convinced you appreciate spiritual values. Your aura may flicker and dim, but in the end, it always glows out bright and clear. For example, yesterday, you gave up ten thousand dollars that Mr Treacle would have given you for the Blue One so that we might worship him and help him change the world. Now, if you do that....'

'I know, I know,' Hercules snarled at him, 'but this time, it's big money.'

The monk looked up at the ceiling as if he were telling it how evil a world it was.

'You and the nun flattered me for a while,' said Hercules. 'I liked your style, and I fell for your wild ideas. I played along with you to the tune of ten thousand dollars. I didn't say I wouldn't steal back the blue cat.'

'Was that ten million for you, Hercules, or you and Virgil until half a minute ago.' said Cleopatra. 'Even if you got your ten million, I wouldn't take any part of it. Nobody, including that crazy blue cat, could ever make my brain go soft. So, I wouldn't ever accept anything from you, Hercules - never again.' She turned to me. 'You'll find Mr Treacle behind the counter in the Bug-Eyed Bar at the All-Pleasures Amusement Park. I'll take you to the exact spot.'

A calm, scornful voice spoke from the dining room. 'And we'll be coming along too.' Standing in front of Zen's altar, his bulging forehead wrinkled with unsmiling amusement was Ralf. To his left stood Florian, eyes gleaming. To Ralf's' right, lounged Wolfgang, yawning but watchful. They were trying to look like the muzzles of the weapons they held. A little behind them stood Judy.

'We've been finding out a lot of things about this blue cat,' said Ralf. 'It would be a lot more desirable if we were the ones who sold it to Uncle Sam. Isn't that so, Judy?'

Judy said nothing. She looked pale, tight-lipped, and miserable for a girl enjoying an act of revenge.

Ralf continued. 'She came whimpering to us, asking us to kidnap Mr Tillet or something silly like that. Can you imagine she was stupid enough to think we'd do something for her after we'd kicked her out of the Kummerspeck Gang? Well, instead of that, she did something for us.'

Judy was looking at me and trying to speak but couldn't get her mouth open. Wolfgang noticed too and twisted her wrist while watching her face.

'There's nothing more to say,' said Ralf. 'You and you and you,' he stabbed a gun muzzle at Hercules, Virgil and the monk. 'You are staying here with my friend Florian. Judy will be here too - in case you get any funny ideas. The rest of you are coming along on a thrill-packed trip to All Pleasures.'

Cleopatra got up with a sullen expression. Cosmo, for once, was silent. I wondered whether Captain Trips and Celeste had avoided the Germans. Then, finally, the nun picked up the dolls depicting Mr Treacle and Dr Womack, put them in a large handbag, and announced, 'Well, I'm ready.'

XIX

THIRD MILLENNIUM THRILLS!

1000 FEET OF FREE-FALL!

YOUR MIND CLEARED IN TEN MINUTES!
Relive Your Childhood

TEST YOUR STRENGTH!

THROW ROCKS AT GLAMOR GIRLS!

FLUORESCENT TATTOOS!

The billboards flared and glared at me as The Germans marched us across the springy, rubberized grounds of All Pleasures Amusement Park. The government crack-down on Love Incorporated had produced a few tangible changes in Double AP, as far as I could judge from my last visit. The burlesque jukeboxes were padlocked, shrouding the rubber figures that would shimmy for a penny. Dresses were an inch higher than usual on the bosoms of the girls working in concessions. There weren't any shifty-eyed gents recruiting special parties to meet a gambling robot or enjoy other forms of illegal entertainment. In front of the sides, someone was painting out the sign that read, 'See the Woman with Four Mammary Glands!' I noticed Cosmo looking up at this defacement.

Yet, there was an uneasiness in the park. Barkers called out too much and stopped too soon. Customers hesitated in front of concessions, shuffled on. Over-age glamour girls ready to dodge rubber rocks, or have their bedclothes or skirts jerked off when

Space Balls hit their planet-simulating target, were a trifle hysterical in the challenges they shrilled at passing patrons.

The fall of Love Incorporated had caused people who treasured their thrills, or the money to be made from them, to say, 'What next?' President McCarthy's rambling apocalyptic speeches had taken effect. The government directive now being barked from the public news-speakers was for the destruction of all cats. This had given people a 'We'd be safer at home' feeling. Or it may have been that the uneasiness at Double AP was part of general anxiety gripping the country. A sense that had been gathering power in the unconscious and was now about to burst in. Something was happening that even the government couldn't handle.

Ralf and Wolfgang shepherded their unwilling assistants through the pupil of one of the surrealistic eyes that served as the entrances to the Bug-Eyed Bar. The gaudy tavern was emptier than the Park outside. Its famous Ten-G Highballs and Stun-Gun Cocktails were going begging. Its drink-hungry hostesses were conspicuous by their absence. The only two customers were being served soda pop by the shorter of the two bartenders, making it simple for Cleopatra, the nun, Cosmo, and I to climb onto the barstools in front of the other bartender. Ralf and Wolfgang stood close behind us.

I couldn't believe the man in front of us was Mr Treacle. His hair looked red, even to the stubble on his cheeks and chin. The eyes he had always kept behind dark glasses were small and squinting like a pig. Although the fugitive from the FBI must have recognized several of us, he didn't show it in any way I could discern. Instead, he looked us all over, polished the bar with a soiled towel and smiled.

'What's your pleasure?'

Ralf's gun dug in my ribs.

'Mr Treacle, I want my blue cat,' I croaked.

Mr Treacle wrinkled his forehead.

'With creme de menthe, chartreuse, or blue fire?'

'I mean my real-life blue cat,' I said.

'I'm sorry. We don't serve drunks here,' said. Mr Treacle 'You've had one too many? What would you ladies and gentlemen care for?'

The nun opened her handbag and laid the Mr Treacle doll on the counter before her. She contemplated it then took off its tiny dark glasses. Its eyes were piggy. She smiled. She replaced the glasses and fished out of her handbag a hatpin, a pair of scissors, a small knife, a tiny pair of pliers, a sample size flame-pack, a small iron with insulated handle, and a white crusted black bottle, and lined them up in a neat row.

'This isn't a powder room, madam,' said Mr Treacle. 'Order your drinks.'

I couldn't help but be impressed by the big man's composure.

Then without warning, I felt a gust of terror. I could tell the blast had hit Mr Treacle, too, for the big man dropped the towel and backed up against the shelves of bottles behind him.

 'Mr Treacle,' said the nun. 'You stole the Blue cat, whom my husband adores. You are going to suffer until you return him.' Her voice shook a little at first, then settled down to a cold, cruel monotone. 'I'm sorry I couldn't bring my travel rack and iron maiden, but these implements are adequate.' She ignited the flame-pack and held the tiny iron over it.

Cleopatra drew her in and Ralf gave a funny grunt. The end of the iron grew red. The nun turned the doll over on its face and dabbed it with the iron, so its pants smoked.

Mr Treacle gasped. He grabbed at the doll, but the nun closed her hand around it. Mr Treacle's arms clamped down against his sides and stayed there. The nun stood the doll up. Mr Treacle straightened. She moved it away from her a few inches. Treacle backed up into the shelves. Sweat beaded his forehead. The nun flicked the doll on the cheek with the hot iron, and Mr Treacle gasped again in pain.

'This sort of thing is going to go on until you give us the Blue cat,' said the nun. A red spot appeared on Mr Treacle's ashen cheek.

 'It's going to get much worse fast,' she said, reaching for the white crusted bottle. Mr Treacle muttered something, but she clamped the thumb of the hand holding the doll over its tiny mouth.

'After a while, I'll be much more likely to trust the things you say,' she explained. Mr Treacle's face grew red, and his eyes bulged.

A shadow came strolling along the top of the bar. It was blue and silken and had a wise face. In a split second of realization, I knew that Zen had opened Mr Treacle's mind and built a bridge between it and the nun. No other unpleasant things were going to happen to Mr Treacle. No one was going to cause any trouble, and all terror vanished. Friendliness and invincible goodwill poured out of Zen, like Scotch from a bottle. There were little sighs and chuckles everywhere. The nun's finger shrank from the white crusted bottle, and she swept all the implements off the bar into her bag. Zen stood in front of me and stretched, working his neck and back muscles. Mr Treacle beamed at the blue cat, and the happy creases around his little piggy eyes looked like those of Santa Claus.

I reached out my hand and stroked the silky blue fur.

'You sure rescued Mr Treacle just in time,' I told Zen, scratching behind his ears.

Mr Treacle straightened up and boomed out, 'What'll it be, friends? The drinks are on the house!'

And they were, too - several quick, cheerful rounds of them. Even Zen got a cocktail of milk, egg white, powdered sugar, and gin. Mr Treacle put it behind the bar on my advice so Zen could sip it in private.

Wolfgang let out an adolescent guffaw and handed two guns, butt-first, to Mr Treacle.

'Reckon I better check my shooting arms,' he said, adapting his German accent to cowboy lingo. Mr Treacle accepted them, tested one by shooting out a light in the ceiling, and put them away. Likewise, Ralf gave up his weapons, with the added instruction that Mr Treacle was to sell them and use the money to buy more liquor when the bar gave out.

With a considerable whiskey in front of her, Cleo leaned across me and said, 'From now on, I'll believe every word every lunatic tells me, especially you.'

As customers drifted into the bar in ones and twos, Mr Treacle called them to join the party. Soon they did and became as friendly and glowing as anyone else. After a time, there was a small crowd, and Mr Treacle did nothing but pour, shake, and serve.

The nun broke away from Cosmo, picked up the Treacle doll, hugged and kissed it, saying, 'You dear, dear man.' he paused, shut his eyes and quaked.

Zen came out from under the bar, jumped on it, and walked up and down in a lordly way but with a definite lurch. He jumped down in front of the bar after a bit, and the crowd parted for him. The drunken blue creature zigzagged with dignity toward an exit.

Mr Treacle heaved himself over the bar, spilling several drinks, and called out, 'Come on, everyone, let's have some fun! Everything at Double AP is free!'

And so, a bacchanalian procession wove through All Pleasures Amusement Park, with Mr Treacle serving as Bacchus. The procession grew larger. Treacle was enjoying himself with godlike capacity. He skipped like a lamb on the rubberized surfacing. He had a word and a joke for everyone and could always offer a new stunt to cap his last.

Cleopatra threw an enormous arm around my neck, almost knocking my head off, and said, 'Got troubles, Maurice? Give them to Mama Cleo, and she'll throw them away. Oh boy, do I love that blue cat! He's got the best little formula for living there is. But, hey, look at it!'

She was pointing at Ralf and Wolfgang, who had discovered a carnival store titled in flaming red phospho-flare KICK THE LOVELY LADY INTO YOUR ARMS and were struggling for the possession of an enormous mallet which had something to do with the game. The game was the age-old one of striking a target on the ground, which caused an indicator to jump up a pole—with the typical late-twentieth-century addition that if the needle reached the top of the pole, not only did a bell ring and lights flare, but a vast hinged lower leg with a cushioned boot swung down and lifted a lovely lady off a perch three feet above the winner and into their arms if they were ready to catch her.

The two happy Germans took many mighty thumps at the target. The indicator jumped high but always hesitated, short of the top. The onlookers sighed. Most of the bacchanalian procession had gathered around the 'kick the lady' concession by this time. Between two bars and opposite the 'Mind Clearers,' they labelled themselves in blinking red fluorescents and a dismal cavern mouth called 'Pluto's Palace,' beside which was an inaccurate solar system model planets revolving.

Mr Treacle was refreshing himself with a pitcher of beer. Two black shapes came undulating in from the outskirts in pursuit of a blue flash. Zen returned to his proper position, bringing the other felines with him.

Ralf tossed the mallet with an amiable grin of defeat. Cosmo came charging up and grabbed if. He stripped off his jacket and shirt, revealing a hairy chest and back.

'Cosmo sure is hairy looking,' The nun murmured to me. 'With those cute ears, he's like a satyr.'

 Cosmo flexed his impressive muscles, took up the mallet, and crashed it down with a force that could rattle teeth. The bell clanged, the light flashed, and the enormous foot descent.

Pandora pushed out of the crowd from the direction of Pluto's moving toward Zen with the single-purposeless of a sleepwalker.

Cosmo sprang upon Pandora, crushing her to his hairy chest, suffocating her with kisses. She was now within range of Zen's influence and pursed her lips at him. He pushed her away from him with a burst of furious anger. Before anyone could stop him, Cosmo snatched up the mallet and brought it down with a titanic crash on the head of the gorgeous violet blonde.

'I was in love with a robot!' he screamed and continued to batter the beautiful head and body, so it bounced up and down on the rubber.

The blue cat, sitting in front of me, seemed to look on with approval.

Pandora writhed between blows and sang, "kiss me honey, honey kiss me," in a high-pitched voice. Her head, flattened by repeated blows, split open. But instead of brains, there was glass, plastic, and metal fragments with wires attached. Then, finally, her voice rose in a final meaningless duck quack, and she stopped moving.

In my mind, several realizations fitted themselves together at this proof Pandora was not a human being but the most advanced of mannequins created by Love Incorporated. Why even her name was a pun from Greek mythology, the metal maiden constructed if I remembered Dr Womack correctly. A woman at the command of Zeus.

As Cosmo put down the mallet, a girl in slacks broke out of the crowd and grabbed my arm. It was Judy Womack, panting and dishevelled.

'Hercules and Virgil,' she panted. 'We got away, but they've gone to warn Mr Brimstone.'

Looking around, I realised they had done just that. Standing in the gloomy entrance to Pluto's Palace was Mr Brimstone, flanked by a half dozen gleaming sales robots. Only these sales robots had gun muzzles jutting from their gleaming turrets.

'Any funny business from anyone, and they mow down the crowd,' Mr Brimstone called, his fingers poised over a box. 'Pandora, stun the blue cat and bring it here.'

The crowd sucked back to either side, and Mr Brimstone saw the wreckage of Pandora, with Zen sitting beside it. Horror came to Mr Brimstone's face. I sensed the golden wave of peace coming from Zen. Mr Brimstone held up his laser and fired.

The blue beam splattered molten rubber a dozen feet from Zen and did no other damage before it winked out. But as the sparkle died,

I saw the beam's backfire had found a target. Mr Brimstone pitched forward with a large hole in his head.

As if Mr Brimstone's fall had been a cue, a small, fattish man stepped out through the curtains of the Mind Clearers. Although he was wearing a sort of partial gas mask, I recognized Dr Womack. He pointed a stun gun. Zen collapsed and was still. The night shifted in a finger snap to a churning terror, which seemed to take the form of a palpable vibration, a wailing roar.

Womack darted forward toward Zen. Besides, the nun jerked something from her pocketbook and waved it in the air.

'Womack!' she screamed, and when the psychiatrist looked her way, she swung the doll of him against her foot, so its head snapped against her heel.

Dr Womack pitched forward on his face. The wailing roar had been a dozen squad cars, converging on the spot from all directions and rocket braking so close it singed the crowd. Men piled out and barked the group into a semblance of control. The man who'd jumped from the foremost car lowered the stun gun with which I'd knocked out Womack.

It was Special Agent Stone.

Out from behind the FBI man stepped Captain Trips, peering about with great interest. I realised this was a world in which you couldn't even trust noble-looking old scientists pretending to be great liberals and babbling government secrets to win your confidence.

I held out my wrists for the handcuffs.

XX

A half-hour later, I had been exposed to so many sets of security checks I guessed there were only two places in the country I could be headed for: the Heptagon or the White House Junior in New Washington. I had been prodded, thumped, scanned, sampled, and subjected to other indignities. My footprints, retinal blood vessel layout, and different physical patterns and dimensions were taken to check against my FBI dossier. I had been X-rayed and tested for bombs. They had checked my blood for germs and viruses. I had been Geiger countered. Lights had flashed in my eyes; questions had dried in my ears. Once or twice, they had put me to sleep. Throughout the process, I was miserable.

A final rubber hand sliding in a slot in the wall hurried me down a corridor and deposited me at the entrance to a large room.

I didn't care anymore.

I was conducted to a seat by a human usher. I looked around. Everyone I had mixed with in the past few days was here: Hercules and Cleopatra Jones, looking amazed, along with Virgil; Mr Treacle with his incongruous red hair; Judy Womack and her father, pale and dizzy; The monk and the nun; Country Joe and Arthur Brown from the institute; Cosmo and Celeste, the latter with a cloak huddled around her; even Ralf, Florian, and Wolfgang. Along with them were quantities of unfamiliar faces—FBI people, I supposed. Guards lined the walls.

Most of these individuals watched three men seated like judges behind an enormous desk across the room: Captain Trips, President McCarthy, and J. Robert Oppenheimer, head of the FBI.

Oppenheimer looked thin, and his face showed an intense and ceaseless curiosity. Still, his interest never became carefree as if each added fact were, for him, an extra responsibility.

Oppenheimer spoke to Special Agent Stone, who was supervising two white-smocked technicians holding a low walled box between banks of electronic tubes and transistors. Inside it, Zen was limp as a dishcloth. Stone had voiced concern about the setup's safety. Still, the research division guaranteed the low-intensity stun field would keep the blue cat harmless.

I heard only the tail end of the conversation as I was seated between Country Joe and the monk. The room fell silent. Oppenheimer looked them all over.

'You all know why you're here. I want the fullest cooperation from everyone. Within the walls of security now surrounding us, complete frankness is possible. I shall be as frank as I expect you to be.'

Oppenheimer paused, leaned forward a little.

'The creature known as the blue cat is real. Its powers of influencing emotion are real. It intends the conquest of the country and the entire world. It is neither mutant nor mechanism but an invader from the planetary system of another star. Captain Trips, will you outline the information you have got from the being known as Celeste?'

Captain Trips' voice was faint but unmistakable.

'The eighth planet of the Star Vega is much like earth though of greater mass. Its landscape, Ms Celeste tells me, can be pictured as endless, hard-baked plains dotted with small lakes and marshes and groves of tall trees. On this planet, intelligent life evolved a swift, hoofed, biped leaf eater whose forelegs became specialized organs for manipulating branches and for brief food-seeking climbs. This specialization occurred when the creature was a primitive equine, so while its hind legs were developing horse-like hoofs, its forelegs were becoming humanoid hands. The result was a being like the satyrs and fauns of Greek mythology. Ms Celeste, would you care to give these people an idea?'

Celeste whipped off her cloak and stood facing them in hirsute nudity. There was no reaction, then she stamped her hoofs twice, and her figure became real. Finally, she wrapped the cloak around her and sat.

'Ms Celeste tells me clothing is not customary on Vega Eight,' Captain Trips observed. 'They have advanced farther than we in technology, possessing force fields that divert gravity and direct atomic drive spaceships capable of approaching the speed of light. But the most remarkable fact about this satyr race is they are symbiotes, and their symbiotic partners are creatures that never evolved on Earth and have a way of life with which we are unfamiliar. So, I will say nothing about these symbiotic partners, except they have no technology and did not originate on Vega Eight. They are not intelligent but handled the Vegan invasion of Earth.'

Captain Trips ignored the murmurs greeting these paradoxical statements.

'Under the urging of their symbiotic partners, the satyrs - if I may use the term - sent a craft to Earth. I gather the 26 light-years were covered in something like two thousand years, though, of course, the time was much less to the voyagers. Approaching Earth, they put their ship into an orbit and rendered it invisible. They stayed in the boat for two more years, except for careful exploratory trips in a gravity-diverting space dinghy. They monitored our TV broadcasts and learned something about our languages and customs. The satyrs discovered it would be possible to disguise themselves as earthlings and did so since they knew it would be desirable to keep in close contact with their scatter-brained symbiotic partners.

'And now,' Captain Trips said. 'I come to where I must describe the symbiotic partners, and I'm not too sure I can.'

Captain Trips shut his eyes.

'You know a pet can bring harmony into a home. Imagine an animal specialized for this purpose and evolving into a harmony bringer. Based on its charm, the cat has established itself in our culture, and imagine how much more successful it would be to bring us beauty, harmony, and peace. Imagine that developing the power to create and spray hormones would dispel anger and create amity in other creatures like the flowers evolved scents and odours to attract the bees. And of it developing, for self-defensive purposes, hormones to create terror. Imagine it gaining extrasensory perception and sensitivity to waves and discovering in this way a whole new realm of possibilities for bringing harmony and making peace. Imagine it becoming what we might call an ESP catalyst, either by acting as an ESP relay station amplifying and redirecting waves or by receiving, copying, and projecting clouds of punched memory molecules. Imagine it surviving and multiplying because it paid for the peace and emotional rapport it brings. We pay the cat for its beauty with food, fondling and protection. Such a creature wouldn't develop general intelligence because it would always depend for its survival on the care of others. Yet, it would have high intelligence in manipulating moods in other animals. It would....'

He hesitated, and Celeste called to him, '... play by ear!'

'Thank you,' said Captain Trips. 'It would always be a transmitter, not the originator. But although lacking general intelligence, it would always seek beings with the highest possible general intelligence since they could bring it the greatest security. It would be cunning in all deceptions enabling it to penetrate a new culture, such as imitating similar appearing animals for camouflage. Like any other species, it would strive to multiply and colonize to fulfil its destiny. Employing its extrasensory powers, it would spy out intelligence in distant places, even distant planets, and persuade its symbiotic partners to take it to those places and planets.'

He paused. 'And now I want all of you,' he said. 'To imagine what it would be like to be the symbiotic partners of such a harmony bringing creature, to have a telepathy of feelings and understanding with those around you, to have a constant guard against those moments of blind rage or selfishness that leads to murder and war, to be always in tune - and yet not deprived of your basic faculties and insights and powers.'

Again, he paused.

'But I don't have to show you. You're in that state of being right now. You are all symbiotes of the blue cat. In a way, you are all blue cats.'

I saw Zen lifting his head over the edge of the box.

'Is all good!' Celeste shouted, jumping up. And with that, the whole solemn meeting melted into a tumbling flood of questions and answers, called insights, babbling conversation.

I heard the monk explaining to Arthur Brown the blue cats were all offspring the ancient Egyptian cats - the Atlantean - had taken the blue cats to Vega.

I heard Virgil grilling the nun about falling for a satyr, and she assured him she went for men with hoofs and was going to make a doll of him.

I heard Hercules pointing out to Dr Womack now they had the blue cat, there would not be too much use for psychoanalysts or police and commissars, and Dr Womack was reminding him most of the commodities peddled by Love Incorporated, including male-female wrestling, wouldn't have much of a market either.

I heard Ralf, Florian and Wolfgang talking about organizing a chivalric order called the Knights of the Blue Cat.

I heard Cleopatra Jones telling Mr Treacle that she'd always liked animals better than humans since her childhood. Mr Treacle explained to her in reply he'd spent so much time getting the jump on people he'd never learned to love them -while poor old Mr Brimstone jumped around.

I heard J. Robert Oppenheimer and Special Agent Stone talking blue cat logistics - would they ever blanket the entire world with the creatures?

I heard Captain Trips and Country Joe talking about something way over my head about ESP-nexuses and lines, and which galaxy did the cats come from in the first place?

While drinking in all this information, I moved through the churning crowd in a definite direction and purpose. I took Judy

Womack's tired hand and assured her that I loved her.

I approached the low walled box from which Zen was still peering in a friendly manner, his eyes like soup spoons large and luminous. I saw myself mirrored in them. But it didn't appear to look like me at all. At first, I did not try to make out exactly who or what I looked like because it was pleasant and soothing to lose myself in the cool pools of Zen's eyes. So calm and clear that it seemed like swimming in a deep lake. It felt delightful to be there, bathed in the beautiful colour and surrounded by warmth. Sometimes the picture would be hazy, and then it would grow relatively straight-forward so that I could see how the shape of my head had altered and not only the body but the colour. My fur now seemed to be relatively short, straight and blue. 'I said 'fur' instead of hair,' I murmured to myself. 'What a strange thing to do. The cat's eyes must be showing me what I look like as a cat.' I found that I could not take my gaze anywhere else.

When the image grew hazy, it seemed to quiver as though things were happening to it from inside. Each time it rose clear, I noticed new details, the light-blue slanted eyes, the nose that had changed into a blue triangle leading to a mouth that was no more like mine than anything I could think of. It curved downwards over long, sharp teeth and sprouted sets of enormous, bristly whiskers from either side. My head was square, my eyes large and staring, and my sharp-pointed ears stood up like antennae. And then I closed my eyes because the image of myself was now so clear and un-mistakable that it was frightening. When I opened them again, it seemed as if I had broken the spell of Zen's cat's-eye mirror. Finally, I avoided staring into it and instead managed to look down at my paws. They were pure blue, large and furred, with quaint, soft pads on the underside and claws curved like swords and needle-sharp at the end.

I saw that I was no longer standing next to the box but inside it —my whole body, long and slender. From ear-tip to tail-tip, I was clad in spotless blue fur. Zen, with his smile and staring eyes, had worked this mischief on me. He nuzzled up against my neck.

The human me had vanished and was nowhere to be seen. Instead, there was only President McCarthy, ten times larger than he had ever appeared before, standing over the box shouting in a voice so loud that it hurt my ears.

'There are two blue cats in here. What is going on?'

'I've seen that other one before,' said Agent Stone. 'It's a fake.'

'I'll take it,' said a female voice. 'I know this is a cosmic crisis and all, but I think it's pretty obvious it's a dye-job.'

Judy's hand gripped my paw, and I jumped out of the box into her arms.

'...I was about to say,' McCarthy finished. 'It's pretty obvious it's a dye-job.'

Judy looked down at me, cradled in her arms. She licked the centre of her upper lip with the tip of her tongue. 'I knew you were important,' she said.

Lightning Source UK Ltd.
Milton Keynes UK
UKHW010252140223
416945UK00006B/575